Stolen Words

Also by Amy Goldman Koss

★

Smoke Screen

More AG Fiction for Intermediate Readers

★

Sister Split
by Sally Warner

★

Letters to Cupid
by Francess Lantz

★

Nowhere, Now Here
by Ann Howard Creel

★

A Ceiling of Stars
by Ann Howard Creel

★

A Song for Jeffrey
by Constance M. Foland

★

Going for Great
by Carolee Brockmann

Stolen Words

Amy Goldman Koss

American Girl

Published by Pleasant Company Publications
Text Copyright © 2001 by Amy Goldman Koss
Cover Illustration Copyright © 2001 by Jean-Claude Götting

Visit our Web site at **www.americangirl.com**

Printed in the United States of America.
First Edition
01 02 03 04 05 06 RRD 10 9 8 7 6 5 4 3 2 1

The characters and events portrayed in this book are fictitious.
Any similarity to real persons, living or dead, is coincidental
and not intended by the author.

AG Fiction™ and the American Girl logo are trademarks of Pleasant Company.

Library of Congress Cataloging-in-Publication Data
Koss, Amy Goldman.
Stolen words / by Amy Goldman Koss.—1st ed.
p. cm. "AG fiction."
Summary: In her diary, eleven-year-old Robyn describes her family's
visit to Austria, from the disastrous theft of their luggage to adventures in the
countryside, while she tries to recover from the death of her Aunt Beth.
ISBN 1-58485-376-X (pbk.)   ISBN 1-58485-377-8 (hc)
[1. Austria—Fiction. 2. Death—Fiction. 3. Aunts—Fiction.
4. Diaries—Fiction.] I. Title.
PZ7.K8527 So 2001
[Fic]—dc21
2001022149

Thanks to Andrea Weiss, Susan Silk,
Clara Rodriguez, Claudia Puig Kronke, and
Emily Koss for their wise counsel;
to Alexandra and Christl Lieben for their
gracious hospitality; and to
Harriet Goldman for her stories

To the memory of my Aunt Mary

I,
Robyn Gittleman,
dedicate this diary
to the memory of my
real diary, which was
stolen.

when: July 12, 4:00ish
where: Hotel in downtown
Vienna, Austria

$\mathcal{I}$ can *write* it: My diary was stolen two and a half hours ago.

And I can *say* it. (I just did, as a matter of fact, and Dad looked up at me.)

But I can't *believe* it. What kind of rotten fruit would steal a total stranger's luggage?

It's not fair! The whole idea of this trip was to cheer ourselves up and sort of bring our family back to life. And I think it was working, maybe, a little. Until that curdled milk stole all our luggage and ruined everything.

I'm trying not to hate Vienna, but it's hard, and I can't help thinking that everyone I see is *him* (or her, or it, or whatever)—that spoiled meat of a crook.

Dad says I should back up and rewrite some of

1

what I wrote in my real diary, at least the stuff since we got to Europe. But I don't even want to *think* about it, much less see it on paper. When I remember that just last night I took a bubble bath in that royal tub, put on the fluffy hotel robe and slippers, and sat at the shiny desk, writing in my *real* diary— it makes me want to SCREAM!!!

When we checked out of the hotel this morning, the plan was to see some sights before moving to the next hotel. So we put our luggage in the rental car and took off for the Emperor's Summer Palace.

The rest is history. We got back to the car after the tour, and Dad said, "Someone broke in!"

I thought he was kidding.

I looked in the back seat. Then I checked the trunk. Then I looked in the back again. And the front again.

I didn't get it. Where was everything?

I told my dad that we must have left our stuff in the hotel lobby this morning—OOPS! The bell-hop was probably scratching his head, wondering why those crazy Americans drove off without their bags. I figured we'd go back to the hotel, find our luggage, smack our heads, and say, "Boy, are we dummies!"

But Dad said there was no chance of that. He told me not to worry, though. He said we'd go straight to the police, and they would be able to help us.

I believed him, and I didn't doubt for a second that our luggage would be returned. I only wondered how I was going to feel about my toothbrush and underwear, knowing that some slime-dog had pawed through them.

In cartoons, cops go tearing after the bad guys and no one even stops to go to the bathroom until justice has been done. But the Viennese police officer just gave Dad a form to fill out and said he was sorry. PERIOD.

My little brother, Joey, told everyone within earshot—English-speaking or not—that his Game Boy and all his action figures were gone. But the Austrian cops *still* didn't spring into action.

So we just huddled, stunned stupid, in the police station, making people walk around us. By then my brother was crying and my mom was sighing.

That was about the time my brain shifted from thinking about everything being gone to thinking about what "everything" meant: MY DIARY! The one that Aunt Beth gave me! That knocked the wind out of me.

Mr. Optimism (Dad) was scrambling as usual to find the silver lining. "Look at it this way," he told us. "We'll have less luggage to lug. And you kids'll have much more leg room in the back seat!"

But I wasn't listening to him.

I was hearing Aunt Beth last Hanukkah, when she gave me the diary. "No one knows what you'll write on these pages," she'd said. "But whatever it is will be yours forever."

She was wrong. My diary is as gone as she is.

I looked at my mother, standing like a zombie in the police station. If anything like this had happened in the old days, Mom would have pitched a holy fit and had the entire city of Vienna out searching for our stuff. But all she managed now was to hang her head and contemplate her toes.

Maybe she thought that the missing part of herself might be on the police station floor, the part that would have let her react like a normal person.

If you were my real diary, I wouldn't have to tell you about the car accident that killed my aunt Beth back in February, with Mom sitting right next to her. You'd already know that's why my mother isn't herself. Or rather, why she's *this* self instead of her old self.

After my dad was finished filling out forms, he herded us outside, saying, "We'll be fine! Mom has her purse and I have my wallet, so we've got the passports, plane tickets, credit cards," yada, yada. "And what matters is that *we* are OK. Luckily, all we lost were things."

He said that last part as if our "things" were less than litter. Like my diary was just a scrap of paper with scribbles.

That's why I was shocked when he bought *you* before we replaced anything else. If Mom had been herself, she would have insisted on combs and tooth-brushes first. Actually, in a twisty way, I think Dad may have bought you for Mom. She doesn't keep a diary, but Aunt Beth did, and Aunt Beth is—or was—Mom's sister. It makes sense if you really think about it.

Or maybe he just bought you first because there was a stationery store next door to the police station. In any case, here you are. European paper is thinner (no offense), and your cover doesn't look as tough either. But none of this is your fault, I guess.

Anyway, we didn't know what else to do, so we came straight here after the police station. This hotel's lobby is dingy and smells like a basement. It's nothing like the hotel we stayed in last night. But I better get used to it, because this is our home for the rest of the trip. Dad's company paid for the first hotel, because Dad was doing work here, but now that our real vacation has started, we're on our own dime.

The woman at the desk looked at us suspiciously when we said we didn't have any luggage. What did she think? That we'd all escaped from family jail? But she gave us our room key and (no bellhop here) flicked her hand in the direction of the elevator.

The elevator weirded me right out. For starters, it was so dinky that even without suitcases, we had to squish to fit in it. Then we stood, all crammed together, waiting for the door to close. After a ridiculously long time, the hotel lady said something to Dad. He knows more German than the rest of us (which isn't saying much), but he still couldn't understand her.

So finally the lady marched over to the elevator, reached in, and yanked on a big black handle, probably convinced that we were all numskulls. Then the door rattled closed, and with a groan of elevator agony, we lurched to a start—but the elevator walls didn't come with us! ACK! It was a just a metal cage.

We watched the floors slide past us until the cage grunted to a stop. Dad cranked open the door, and we had to step *up* into the hallway. It would be awful to get stuck between floors in any elevator, but it would have been beyond awful in this one. We were thrilled (at least I was) to get out of it and into the room.

This hotel doesn't have fluffy bathrobes with the Austrian flag embroidered on the pocket (sigh). And there will be no more shiny desks packed with hotel stationery and pens, but at least we can close the door on Vienna.

It felt funny to have nothing to unpack.

We just sort of sat down.

Then Dad got on the phone, contacting his office back in the States, telling them about his stolen work stuff. In spite of the fake smile he stuck on his face when he caught me looking at him, Dad seemed mighty frazzled.

He's a manufacturer's rep for an office supply company. From the look on his face, you'd think his briefcase contained top-secret documents about pushpins, or critical information needed to prevent Austria from a crippling paper-clip shortage.

But I suppose Dad is just freaked because his laptop was expensive and all his records are lost.

Between calls, I asked him if his boss was mad. Dad replied, "Nobody is happy about this situation, Robyn. But we'll be fine." Which means, "Mind your own business and leave me alone," right?

But the Austrian businesspeople Dad came here to meet with must not be very mad at him, because they've invited us over for dinner tonight.

We'll have to wear the same things we've been wearing all day. P.U.! But that's all we've got. Joey doesn't care if he wears the same sweaty clothes every single day for the rest of this trip, but I do. And I'm not wild about washing my underwear in the sink every night, either.

P.S. At least Dad went out and bought us new toothbrushes. And he got licorice toothpaste! Is that strange or what? It tastes black, but it's not. Europe is not America.

time: 10:28 p.m.
place: Apartment of Dad's
work friends

Mr. and Mrs. Müller. I've always wanted to write something with those dots. Dad says they're called umlauts. I should add them to my name: Röbyn. Does that look cool or what?

Anyway, we walked here from the hotel. Dad oohed and aahed like a total tourist over every building and fountain. I don't know if he really loves all the curved doorways and curlicues that much, or if he just thinks Joey and I should.

But his enthusiasm didn't work, at least not on me. I was busy dreading bad guys. I could feel them around every corner, about to pounce on us like lions on baby antelope in a PBS documentary.

Plus we still have to walk *back* through bands of

murderous thieves. In the dark. Late at night. And it's getting darker and later. But the grownups keep yakking away without a thought of the dangers awaiting us.

Mom is trying to impersonate a normal person, and the Müllers seem to be falling for it. That's because they don't know what my mother used to be like.

It's even hard for *me* to believe Mom ever threw back her head and laughed like some bizarre tropical bird—but she did.

I remember one school talent show when some kids from my class did a comedy routine, and my mom's wild hooting was the hands-down-loudest laugh in the entire auditorium. I prayed no one knew she belonged to me.

Even Aunt Beth, who was there, told Mom that she might as well have come to school in her nightie, with pink curlers in her hair, if her intention was to embarrass me to death.

Mom ignored Aunt Beth and kept shrieking her crazy-bird laugh.

Well, now my aunt isn't here to tell my mom to quit laughing, but Mom quit anyway.

You know something? I miss Aunt Beth with all my heart, but I miss my mom even more. Including her awful laugh.

I even miss the way Mom used to bite me. Not *hard* or anything, no blood. Sometimes she'd just be giving me a hug and then—ouch! She'd nip like an animal. She'd apologize, then say she couldn't help it because I looked so delicious.

Now look at her, sitting there so stiffly at the table. Can you picture that brittle twig sinking her teeth into me?

And can you believe she's the same person who used to get red-in-the-face furious over my messy bedroom, or torment me about practicing piano?

What would I have to do now to get that kind of reaction? I can barely get Mom's attention, let alone her teeth marks.

Anyway, these Müller people are nice enough, and I love writing their name. But they don't have kids and I'm bored to death and starving. (That sound is my stomach growling.) The dinner *looked* good until Mr. Müller explained that the meatballs were really *liverballs,* and the sausage was *blood* sausage! Can you imagine?

I thought Joey was going to barf on the spot. I filled up on bread and water, like a prisoner, but I'm still hungry.

Now Joey is crashed on the couch. He's drooling. I wish I could just let go like that and sleep anywhere (minus the drool). But I can't. So, here I am. Tired, full of dread, and wasting away from malnutrition on my marvelous European vacation.

later: Midnightish
place: Hotel balcony (great view of a stone wall three feet away)

The good news is: We didn't get mugged or murdered or run over on our way home from the Müllers' inedible dinner. We took a taxicab.

The bad news is: My roll-away cot is made of jagged rocks. I tried lying down on it, but sleep isn't going to happen within ten feet of that collection of lumps. Meanwhile, Joey whined and whimpered about everything under the moon until Dad promised to look for a toy store as soon as he possibly could, just to shut Joey up. It worked, and Joey was snoring (and drooling) within seconds.

I wonder if our thief is sleeping.

Did he give his daughter my new blue skirt, the one I bought for this trip? Did she say, *"Danke"* ("thanks" in German) and kiss him on both cheeks, like they do here?

It kills me that while that blood sausage was ripping us off, we were crunching along on the pebbled walkways of the Emperor's Summer Palace, suspecting ABSOLUTELY NOTHING.

I, for one, was happily imagining princesses drifting through the royal gardens in flowing gowns. The gardens were complicated, lacy patterns of flowers, growing perfectly, without a petal out of line. It was amazing—but it wasn't worth all our luggage.

Why didn't we sense danger? Especially Dad? He travels a lot for work. Shouldn't he have known not to leave our stuff in the car? Why didn't we drop our bags at the new hotel *before* going to the palace?

I̲t's too strange to reach for you and have you be *you* when my real diary is who-knows-where. But I guess you're better than nothing, for now.

One thing (maybe the only thing) I like about Vienna is the breakfast buffet, which is where we are now. Dad, who goes to the gym all the time and complains constantly about his gut, calls the buffet the "Heart-Attack Special" because of all the fattening cream sauces and fried stuff. My mom never has more than a cup of coffee for breakfast, so her opinion—if she actually had one—wouldn't count. And Joey has refused to eat anything besides ice cream since we left Baltimore.

But me . . . mmmm! That glob on the page is apricot jam (sorry).

13

The only problem is that everyone in the restaurant eats quietly but us. Joey can't sit at a table for more than two seconds without knocking over at least five things and falling off his chair with a bang and a shriek. Dad isn't all that dignified, either. He talks louder, I swear, than anyone else in Europe.

Mom is too depressed to be loud, but she's still plenty embarrassing. For one thing, she's jumpy, as if she's constantly surprised to find herself wherever she is. The least sound makes her leap out of her skin. A fork dropped on a plate? Mom hits the roof. A minute ago the waiter came to our table to give Dad the check, and Mom yelped and sloshed her coffee all over the tablecloth.

The other thing is her tears. Back home I was almost used to them. But it's entirely different in a hotel dining room in a foreign country in front of total strangers. At least she's a quiet crier. No sniffling or sobbing. She just twists up her face, and tears leak out.

Mom's friend Susan, who's a shrink, told me a few months ago that Mom was in shock. But how long can this last? On TV, people are in shock for one scene, maybe two—never the whole program.

Interesting development: Dad just announced that the Müllers, in whose apartment we spent an eternity last night, said we could go stay at their farmhouse out in the country!

Mom came to life for a second to say, "That's very generous, but we should stick to our original plan." Meaning, we should stay in this ho-hum hotel and drag ourselves around thief-infested Vienna.

Mom said she's not comfortable accepting favors from strangers.

Dad said the Müllers aren't strangers.

Mom looked like she was going to object some more, but then I watched the will just seep right out of her.

Then Dad leaned toward me and whispered that the Müllers offered us their farmhouse because of *me!* He said that last night when they asked me how I was enjoying Vienna, I shuddered. I honestly don't remember that.

Dad told me that the Müllers were ashamed that I'd been a victim of crime in their country, and they felt it was their civic duty to improve my impression of their homeland.

Now I wish I'd paid more attention to those brilliant people, blood sausage or not. How often does anyone take that kind of interest in my shudders?

Dad says we should all think about the idea this morning while we're sight-seeing, and we'll vote later.

What's to think about? I'm ready to go!

when: Lunchtime
where: Restaurant in the
land of the living

We just got back from Stephansdom, which is an enormous, ornate old cathedral full of terribly serious statues and sad paintings and marble altars with gold everywhere.

Every inch was carved and decorated all the way up, up, up to the vaulted ceilings, where real live pigeons were cooing and pooing. I'm sure they weren't supposed to be there, but the gigantic doors had been left wide open, so the pigeons must have just flown in.

I wandered around imagining horror-movie music coming out of the incredible pipe organ. Then Dad pointed to a bench and said it was an aboveground grave, a crypt. ICK! He showed me a whole bunch of them right there inside the church. He said they were full of dead bishops and priests and members of the aristocracy.

In case that wasn't gruesome enough, there were tunnels twisting underground with burial chambers called catacombs, and there were tours every hour! I couldn't resist lining up for that.

Joey begged to go along, but he always thinks he can handle stuff like that—and then he gets screaming nightmares and keeps the whole family awake. So Mom stayed behind with him.

Our guide, a short, gray-haired man with bushy eyebrows, was a little too enthusiastic about his job, if you ask me. He gave his talk first in German for everyone else on the tour, and then he translated it into English so Dad and I would know what was so funny about everything he was saying.

Nothing was funny tee-hee. More like funny gross. For instance, in the first room, the guide said, "Anyone care for tinned meat? Within these jugs are the vital organs—kidneys, hearts, livers, and lungs—of members of the Hapsburg family, children and adults alike. Perhaps not as fresh as they once were, but preserved remarkably nonetheless!"

Next he led us down a gloomy passageway past bones stacked as neatly as Lincoln Logs, saying, "It used to be someone's job to come down and shake off the dried bits of flesh and place the bones in space-saving ways so there'd be room for more."

He said this as if bone-arranging was an extra-creepy career choice—which, of course, it is, but look who was talking!

Then he led us to a jumble of skeletons and told us it was a mass grave for victims of the black plague back in the year seventeen-something. EEEWW!

I was glad Mom wasn't with us. She didn't need to

see all those bones. They would only have made her think of Aunt Beth's. As I stood there studying them, it got hard for me to breathe.

But even gulping like a fish, I still acted more mature than the lady who began giggling in the pickled-kidney chamber and didn't quit until our guide finally brought us to the exit.

With my whole body still sort of humming from the death tour, we found my mom and Joey in the cathedral, looking as teeny as two ants in that enormous space.

As we got closer, I saw that the Joey-ant was scrambling around on the pews with his grubby feet, while the mother-ant sat, as still and pale as the marble saint on the altar.

Joey was still in a twist about being left behind, so when he begged to climb the bell tower, Dad agreed to take him. I went too, because even though I'm not one bit fond of heights, I figured that after the catacombs, anything above ground would be a relief.

Wrong.

The tower was a tightly spiraling stone staircase that seemed to get narrower and narrower, with only a microscopic window now and then. The steps were partly worn away, adding to their overall spookiness.

"Why don't they turn on the stupid lights?" was Joey's question.

I told him to shut up. This had been his idea.

By the time we arrived, panting, at the top, who cared about the view? I, for one, just wanted to be anywhere but there.

And now I am. HALLELUJAH!

We're in a little restaurant with big sunny windows, waiting for our lunch. Schnitzel, of course—flat, deep-fried patties of chicken or veal or whatever. Lunch everywhere is usually either schnitzel or sausage from the wurst (worst?) family. (Bratwurst, knockwurst, liverwurst—*bloodwurst!*) I'm starving, but I'm not complaining about how long it's taking to get our food. I'm just grateful to be breathing regular air, with my feet on solid ground.

Plus, we just voted about the Müllers' farmhouse, and it's settled. We're going!

Before we voted, Dad reminded me of the hours I spent hunting through travel books on Vienna. I'd listed all the places I wanted to see, like museums that sounded cool and, of course, the famous giant Ferris wheel.

But what was I thinking?? Now that I'm here, I remember that the only thing I like about museums is the gift shop. And famous or not, Ferris wheels scare me to death.

As soon as I voted to leave town, Joey canceled out my vote by crossing his scrawny arms and saying with a pout, "There's no way I'm going to any stupid farmhouse! And you can't make me!" Then he stuck his tongue out at me, so I hit him.

I know why he doesn't want to go. Number one, because he never wants to do what I want to do. And number two, he thinks there'll be more toy stores in the city than out in the country.

Dad said that whatever we decided was fine with him, but anyone could tell he was gung ho for the farmhouse.

Then he asked Mom what she wanted.

She cleared her throat, which hadn't been used in a while, and said, "I'd rather not accept favors. But I guess it might be nice to see the countryside." Then she shrugged and looked down at her silverware.

So the good news is: I won! We leave tomorrow. Not for home, unfortunately, but for someplace other than here.

Joey says it'll be all my fault if the place is poopy.

later: Our last night in this hotel room

Mom is sleeping diagonally across the bed. She had one of her cries earlier, and I guess it must have tired her out. I hope her dreams are more fun than her real life.

Dad's on the phone again, naturally.

And Joey's watching an American cowboy movie dubbed into German on TV. The cowboys' mouths stop moving way before they're done talking, but Joey doesn't care.

We went clothes shopping after lunch. Dad was in charge of getting stuff for Joey. No one was in charge of me, except for myself.

As soon as we got to the store, Mom bought herself a blue cotton dress that she didn't even try on, even though the sizes here are marked totally differently than they are in the U.S. Then she stood next to a clothing rack, staring into space and stroking a velvet skirt.

I came out of the dressing room a few times to show her what I was trying on, but all she said was "That's nice, honey," and kept feeling the velvet material. She rubbed it between her fingers as if it were her security blanket.

When you consider all the incredible hair-raising shopping battles that my mother and I used to get into in the pre-accident days, you'd think I would be thrilled that she no longer gives a hoot about what I buy. So I can't really explain why I didn't get anything interesting today. I just bought a nothing-special shirt and a plain pair of jeans, and some underwear and socks.

Speaking of socks, Dad asked a salesman if they carried the kind that keep men's feet from stinking. When the poor guy had no idea what my father was talking about, Dad explained his foot odor problem again, LOUDER.

Meanwhile, my twerpy brother kept himself entertained by hiding in the racks of clothing and popping out to scare people to death.

Did I mention that not a single other shopper either announced that he had smelly feet, or ambushed unsuspecting strangers, or practically rubbed a hole through a skirt that she didn't buy? Needless to say, I pretended to be an orphan, shopping alone.

Which I kind of was anyway.

But at least tomorrow we pack up (now that we have something to pack) and then it's good-bye Vienna! Or *Wein,* as they spell it here.

The only bad thing is that I'll be leaving the last place that I had my real diary. It's not like I believe my diary is out there sniffing doorways and searching the streets for me, but still, I feel like I'm leaving it behind.

I reminded Dad to tell the police where we were going to be, just in case they turn up anything. He said he already did.

I hope so.

2:36 a.m. (!)

These two thoughts woke me—

Thought Number One: What if my diary has fallen into the hands of a mean, English-reading bad guy? What if he's thumbing through the pages right now with his grubby fingers, laughing at me? Reading secret things that no one knows and no one *should* know?

But then Thought Number Two came with a sort of tingle: Maybe after the thief tossed my diary into a trash can, someone else—someone nice—plucked it out, wiped off the crud and crumbs, and took it home. And maybe now that person is reading it. Maybe someone they loved has died. Maybe their whole life is falling apart and the people around them have turned inside out. And maybe my diary is helping them feel less lonely!

It makes my chest feel a little lighter to think that out in the world there might be a total stranger who understands me, who feels like I do. And even if we never meet, at least we'll always know we're not alone.

That probably sounds nuts, and when I read it over in the morning, I'll want to tear the page out. But Aunt Beth told me never, under any circumstances, to edit my diary. She said that was a crime against history.

I wonder if in all her years of journal writing, Aunt B ever lost one of her diaries. Or if she ever showed what she wrote to anybody. If she'd had a husband, would she have let him read it? Will I show mine to my husband someday?

And while we're on the subject, I wonder why Aunt Beth never got married. Everyone liked her— in fact, over the years she brought a whole parade of dates to our house.

Sometimes she'd send them outside to play catch with "Uncle Joe" (that's what she called my brother). Then she'd pull me over to the window to spy on them and grill me for my opinion. She'd ask if the guy's smile seemed slightly sneaky to me, or if I thought there was anything geeky about his shoes. She'd squint at me and say, "Give it to me straight, girlfriend, don't you suspect that he may very possibly have been a salamander in a past life?"

I always said things like "His smile is sweet" or "I love his shoes" or "Salamanders are cute," because I wanted to be her bridesmaid more than anything on earth. I also secretly thought that my aunt would always be so much cooler than any of the men she dated that it hardly mattered which lucky guy was the groom.

I guess it's a good thing now that she didn't marry any of those guys. Otherwise her husband would just be another incredibly sad person whose life is wrecked. Isn't it amazing how many lives can be ruined by a single car accident?

But what if the reason Aunt B didn't get married was because she was destined to meet her one true love next month or next year? And now she won't be able to keep that appointment! Some poor man will spend his life alone, not knowing why he never found his soul mate. That's so sad.

Mom once told me that she felt guilty for living such a perfect life, for having Dad and me and Joey while Aunt Beth had no one. But when I looked at my mother's life compared to my aunt's, it always seemed to me like Aunt Beth was the one who was having all the fun.

date: July 14
time: 10:35 a.m. (which means
4:35 a.m. in Baltimore!)
where: Heading for the Alps . . .
HOORAY!

Too bad we have to take this puny rental car with us. It didn't do a thing to protect our luggage. It just handed everything over without a squawk.

I can't believe how adorable I thought this car was when we picked it up at the airport. I actually wrote (in my real diary) that it was cute. I'd never been in such a teensy car, besides bumper cars at the fair. This rental could curl up on the seat of our minivan at home.

Even little Miss Sweetness Brown, Aunt Beth's '73 Ford Mustang, is—or rather, was—bigger than this one.

Aunt Beth and Miss Sweetness Brown had been together forever. My aunt loved her. She always looked for parking spaces where Miss Sweetness would have the nicest view possible. And my aunt took Miss Sweetness to auto shows to visit with other elderly autos.

It hurts to think of poor Miss Sweetness Brown rusting away, crunched and dusty in some junkyard somewhere.

This stinky little tin can is no Miss Sweetness Brown, that's for sure! Not to mention, Dad can barely drive it. He's not so bad on the *autobahn*. (That's the freeway here, which has no speed limit!) But going uphill, the car stalls and lurches and makes horrible noises. Dad says it's a manual yada-yada, and he's used to driving an automatic yada.

Well, at least we're moving farther and farther away from the crime scene.

And it does sound glamorous to be heading for a country house in the Alps, doesn't it? Plus, guess what—Mrs. Müller told me the farmhouse is *three hundred* years old!

We stopped at her apartment this morning for directions, and she told me I'd love being there. I hope she's right. She also said it would do my mother a world of good. I hope she's right about that, too.

I guess my mom didn't fool the Müllers after all.

It's hard not to be mad at Aunt Beth for doing this to my mom. But that's ridiculous. How can I be mad at Aunt B? Look what she did to herself! Anyway, it wasn't her fault. It was Miss Sweetness Brown's. No, it was the ice. I don't know. Either way, I'm mad.

Speaking of ice, Dad says there's a glacier up ahead of us.

A WHAT???

According to him, you can take a cable car up to see it. No thanks! When my parents dragged me to the slopes two winters ago for my first and last ski trip ever, the part I hated the most was the chairlift to the top, and Dad says this would be much, much higher. FORGET IT.

A glacier is a monstrous, overgrown ice cube, right? So that cable car wouldn't even be dangling over soft, fluffy snow but over ice as hard as rock and colder than the moon.

Well, I hate ice. As a matter of fact, when I grow up I'm moving to a steamy tropical place where they don't even have a word in their language for ice, or snow, or hail, or frost, or sleet, or slush. A place where you can never see your breath and no one even owns a coat.

The whole time I've been trying to write this, Joey has been flapping his lips about what he wishes would happen to our thief.

For example: "I hope the police find him and shoot him right between the eyes. POW!"

Then, since no one from the front seat hushed him, Joey cranked it up to "No, I hope they throw him in jail, and the meanest, ugliest guy there hacks off his arms and beats him to death with them! WHAM!"

In the old days, my parents would have told my brother to can it, right? Well, this time they just nodded like Joey was talking about the weather. Which, by the way, is awful. It started raining when we were leaving Vienna, and it hasn't stopped since.

Ack! My raincoat!!

To be completely honest, I never liked that coat. But that's not the point. The point is, I keep thinking I've remembered everything in my suitcase, but then something else comes to mind, and it's like a slap—smack!—across the face.

Maybe if I list every single solitary item that was stolen, there won't be any more slaps. Here goes:

1) My raincoat
2) My diary—about three-quarters full (of me)
3) My hairbrush with all the ponytail thingies wrapped around the handle
4) My new red sandals with the beads on the straps (which I never even got to wear)
5) My brand new blue skirt and top (also unworn)

This is making me sick. I'll do the rest later. Or maybe never.

Who'd have guessed I'd miss Joey's Game Boy? I used to beg Mom to make him turn the sound off. But right now I'd rather be listening to that awful "music" than his obnoxious babbling.

I do feel a little sorry for Joey, though. Back home, my brother drove himself and everyone else crazy trying to decide which dolls (he hates it when I call them "dolls") should be the lucky winners of the Trip-to-Europe Contest. And now those worthy few are history.

Joey just grabbed you and tried to throw you out the window. I had to pinch him to get you back, and now he's crying like a baby.

I take back everything I wrote. Joey deserved to be robbed.

Dad just pulled the car off the road and made us all get out to look at the glacier in the distance. Our binoculars are gone, of course, but even with bare eyeballs you could tell that the spiky part with snow on it wasn't like the mountains around it. It looked like a huge, jagged bowl of vanilla ice cream.

Traffic whizzed past at a hundred-plus miles an hour, but in between the cars, it was absolutely silent. And I knew that, even before there was a road here, ancient, grunting humans probably looked up and saw the same bowl of ice cream.

After we got back in the car and Dad tried to pull onto the (steep) road, the car rolled backward! What a sickening feeling. Dad was grinding the gears and stomping on the pedals, but the car just kept on rolling. Joey and I screamed. Mom, who should have been more freaked out than anyone, didn't even seem to notice.

Sometimes I want to yell at her, "WHO DIED IN THAT CRASH? YOU OR AUNT BETH?"

Here's what I think: My mom and my aunt left together for the dance concert, and neither of them really came back.

The only thing that Mom ever told me about what happened that night was that Miss Sweetness Brown went into a skid and spun out of control on the icy freeway.

Or maybe Dad told me that.

And that's it. No one would tell me anything else. Nothing.

I did hear some man after the funeral talking about "black ice." Just the sound of that gives me chills. He was saying that it's completely invisible and looks just like a wet road but really it's sheer ice, smooth and clear as glass. A mean trick of nature. An illusion.

I'm going to kiss the ground when I get out of this stinky rental car.

Dad says we should go to take a closer look at that glacier one of the days that we're here. No rush, as far as I'm concerned. Because here's what I know about glaciers: The Titanic hit one and sank. Actually that was an iceberg. But an iceberg is only a little chip of ice compared to a glacier, right?

Here's what else I know: Glaciers are so big that they carve valleys just by moving. And they create lakes and rivers and oceans just by melting a little.

Joey says he's getting carsick. If he barfs on me, I swear I'll wring his wormy little neck!

where: HERE!
when: NOW!

UNBELIEVABLE! Unbelievably GORGEOUS! This place is amazing.

I want to describe every inch of the farmhouse and everything around it—although I know I'll never forget it even if I don't take a single picture or write down a single word.

Let's start with when we got to the top of the long driveway and saw it.

No, I'll start with when we opened the door and surprised the caretaker. She was a tall, skinny woman with shoved-back short hair. We saw her for only one quick second before she hurried away.

Right now, I'm sitting on a deep wooden window seat that's exactly the perfect size for me. Every window in the house has one, and they all have shutters, too! Real ones, like the kind Heidi threw open in that famous movie. You just unhook and push!

And the view *out* the window is so fairy-tale quaint that if you saw a picture of it, you'd think it was fake. We are plunked down in the middle of a field of big white, medium-size blue, and tiny yellow wildflowers. It's exactly the kind of meadow that a person imagines when a person imagines running through a field of wildflowers. And without even turning my head I can see green hills, a twinkly lake, and a towering mountain. Even the sky is perfect— perfectly blue with fat white clouds.

Inside, there's not much stuff. In fact, this room is practically bare. There's nothing in it for decoration except a big white bowl with green squiggles, sitting on a table.

So what makes it so unbelievably pretty?

There are no real closets in any of the rooms. I guess they hadn't been invented when this place was built. So each room has an armoire. That's a huge cabinet with drawers, shelves, and a place to hang stuff. Each armoire is shaped differently. The one in this room (I'm in the dining room) has blue flowers painted in the corners and the year 1424 across the top. That makes it older than the whole U.S.A.!

I just peeked inside. There are stacks of heavy white plates and bowls, all with the same loopy green design on them as the bowl on the table. So maybe that bowl isn't for decoration after all. It just didn't fit in the cabinet.

My Aunt Beth would have loved this. She always said that useful things should be either beautiful or interesting looking, and she didn't want to own anything that wasn't useful. I never really got that until now. I just thought she hated clutter. But this house is exactly what she meant.

What's Joey screaming about?

A cow. Out the side door.

It mooed at him. Joey says it was a mean moo, not a regular, friendly moo. Sometimes he's funny.

Dad has been practically skipping from room to room saying, "Can you believe we're in a place like this?" and "Isn't this incredible?"

This time he's right.

when: A bit later
where: A different window seat

The view from this one is of the orchard full of twisted apple trees. I'm in the library—a room with log-like shelves of books. The ones I leafed through were old and written in either German or French, so all I could do was look at the pictures. That must be how it felt before I could read.

But who needs books when there are views like this one to look at? Just staring out this window is the best possible use of my eyeballs. See how the sunshine through the window is making stripes across the thin, ancient-looking rug?

Actually, this room and the way the light streams in reminds me of those old paintings of women with pitchers of milk that Aunt Beth took me to see at the art museum. Did women like that live here? Did they wear white scarves on their heads and heavy dark skirts that dragged on the floor—right here in this very room?

Dad just came in to show me that he has to duck to fit through the doorway. He said he would have been a big-shot if he'd lived here back when the house was built, because people were shorter then.

Joey followed my dad in here and grumbled, "What's the matter with the stupid floor?"

I told him nothing was wrong with the floor. It was just old.

"Yeah, but look." He was annoyed. "It goes way up on this side, and it's full of bumps."

Joey's right. The floor slants like in a fun house, and the wood is worn smooth, except for the knots, which poke up higher than the rest of the floor. I learned at camp that the knots are the hardest part of a piece of wood. These floors suddenly made that the coolest fact on earth.

Joey was unimpressed. He stomped off after my dad to complain about something else, no doubt. He has decided to hate it here and that's all there is to it. But that's his problem.

There's my shadow on the wall. I just waved to myself. Hi!

Minutes later

I was practically happy, wandering around, loving everything, until I turned down a hallway and there was Mom, staring at a big, black, old-fashioned dial telephone on a table. I know what she was thinking. She wanted to call Aunt Beth and tell her about this place. They used to talk every single day, at least once.

This isn't the first time I've seen Mom get paralyzed by the sight of a phone, but it still sucks the life out of me every time I see it.

Dad came along and pretended not to know that Mom was about to start crying. He said something like, "Let's run into town and get some provisions!"

Rah-rah! I should get my father cheerleading pom-poms.

He wasn't always this way, you know. I mean, he was always sweet, but he was, well . . . busy. *Really* busy, like working late, taking business trips, going to the gym, reading the newspaper, paying bills, watching football, taking more business trips, fixing stuff around the apartment, etc. Dad has always been more around the edges of our family than smack-dab in center stage.

But now I guess he's trying to fill in the hole where Mom's personality used to be. Maybe he thinks that if he acts extra-super-chipper, Joey and I won't notice how extra-super-miserable Mom is.

Anyway, I never want to leave this incredible house, view, or window seat. But everyone's going into town, and they won't let me stay here alone. So, off I go.

when: 3:16 in the Austrian afternoon

I'm back! Did you miss me?

The town is called *Zell am See* and is only a few minutes' drive away. And it's way more twenty-first century than I was expecting, considering that it's a zillion-year-old town in the middle of nowhere.

First we went to the market, which was wacky. There were a million kinds of meat—sausages of all colors and sizes, and the tongues and livers of whole barnyards of animals. Plus milk in bags. Everything was labeled in German, of course. But some things were a cinch to figure out, like *tee* is tea. And most of the cans and boxes had pictures.

After we shopped, Dad ducked into an office place with fax machines and Internet hookups. Even though he's been pretending that the theft of our luggage is no big deal, he still stops at every phone to call the police in Vienna or his office in the States.

You can tell by his clamped jaw that he's stressed to the bone. He reminds me of one of those two-faced action figures Joey has. Except instead of a snarling, iron-masked bad-guy face that flips to reveal a semi-human alien face, Dad's faces are both cheerful. A thin, cracking, exhausted cheerful over an industrial-strength mega-cheerful.

While my dad was zipping through cyberspace, Mom and Joey and I walked around the cobble-stoned town square. Pigeons here look and sound exactly like regular pigeons, which should probably not surprise me but it does.

Joey and I threw pennies into the fountain in the center of the square. My wish—as always—was that Mom would snap out of her funk. I don't know what Joey wished for, but I can guess (toys).

The fountain was across from a church with an onion-shaped dome. The buildings in between had shops and cafés at street level, with sunny yellow-and-white-striped umbrellas. And upstairs there were apartments with laundry flapping merrily on clotheslines strung from window to window.

Laundry at home never looks merry.

There were people walking around actually wearing *Heidi* hats (the kind with the little feather) and *The Sound of Music* clothes. Mom told me that the full-skirted dresses with aprons are called *dirndls* and the men's shorts with suspenders are *lederhosen*. She almost looked happy.

We strolled to the end of the street, and there was a sheep grazing as calmly as you please—as if being a sheep at the end of the street was perfectly normal. Even Mom laughed!

I watched her reach over the fence to pat the sheep's spongy wool. I couldn't help hoping this would be the moment the spell would be broken. Could an Austrian sheep be my mom's magic charm?

I barely breathed, not wanting to ruin it.

Even Joey kept sort of still, for him.

But then Mom said, "Do you remember Ba-Ba?" Of course I do. She didn't wait for my answer. "The stuffed sheep on your Auntie Beth's bed? She had that ratty old thing since she was an infant."

I watched Mom's shoulders sag, and I practically felt my own bones melt like wax.

Here's what I wonder: Does Mom remind herself of Aunt B on purpose, to make sure she never gets happy? Or does she just think about her sister so much that *everything* eventually connects back to Aunt Beth?

I don't get it.

I shook myself and focused my attention back on this storybook town with its sheep and its fountain and its laundry. I tried to imagine living in one of those upstairs flats and pushing my shutters open every morning to a view of the square.

If I had shutters to throw open back home, I'd see the plum tree, or at least what's left of it since last February's storm.

And I'd probably see Richard fussing around in Steven's garden, which is sad but kind of sweet. Steven and Richard lived in the apartment downstairs forever until Steven died. Ever since then, Richard has been trying to keep up Steven's garden. He weeds and waters it and asks the people at the nursery for advice all the time. But still, the garden isn't as nice as it was when Steven was alive.

I'd also see the row houses across the street and the intersection with the four-way stop and its constant traffic jam. I might see the raggedy woman who squeaks a shopping cart up and down, back and forth, looking for cans and bottles.

But I wouldn't see any sheep.

The ride back from town wasn't too bad. Dad managed to get a running start up the hill. He hit the gas and zoom! So we made it home without any backward rolling.

All in all, my dad's cheerleading seems to have worked. Joey is as happy as a clam because we found action figures in a little toy shop on the square. Now he can shoot to his heart's content.

And Mom seems a little less gloomy because she has something to do (put away groceries). But when Dad was going on and on, all excited about the farmhouse, I heard him say to Mom, "Look around you, Debby! Isn't this remarkable?"

And my mom answered, "It's bigger than I'd anticipated."

Dad let his everything-is-great face slip for a split second and allowed a hint of exasperation to show. "That's all? It's bigger than you anticipated?"

Mom blinked at him. "It's pretty?" she said, as if guessing an answer on a pop quiz.

I try to imagine what she would have said about this place . . . before. I bet she would have twirled in the front hall and laughed her shrieking parrot laugh. It would have been her, not Dad, running from room to room pointing at things. And she'd probably have grabbed me in her excitement and squeezed me so hard it would have knocked the wind out of me.

No one has hugged me like that in a long time.

I suppose there's no point in thinking about "what would have been" if everything had been different. And yet, it's kind of nice in an awful sort of way—or it's awful in a nice sort of way.

when: Evening
where: At the top of the house

Since Joey and I have been sharing a hotel room for the last three nights, Mom thought it would be a good idea for us to sleep in the same room *here*, too! I refused, and luckily Dad backed me up. Mom backed down.

Joey followed me around, calling dibs on every room I looked interested in. So I told him that he had to pick first and stick to his choice. Then we went through all the rooms again. I didn't let on that the topmost room was my favorite until after Joey had picked the one with the swing hanging from a beam.

But then my dad told Joey that he had to sleep in the room next to theirs in case he needed them during the night. So none of our dibs or deals mattered anyway.

Now I'm way up on the fourth floor, in my dream room. The ceiling comes to a point, and the walls slope down to the window seats—definitely the best room in the house.

Bedtime

There was no moon tonight, no streetlights, no city glow. Nothing outside these windows but darkness. I closed the shutters.

I'm in bed now, and it's as quiet as can be. The walls are so thick in this house that you couldn't hear a person scream in the next room, let alone three floors down. (Not that I'm going to scream or anything.) But it's so QUIET up here I can hear my own pulse.

Joey's sure this house is haunted.

I never did believe in ghosts, but I believe in them even less since Aunt Beth died. That's because if dead people could come back to haunt us, I'm sure Aunt B would have visited us by now, just to say hi. She wouldn't be able to resist freaking me out and making a joke out of it.

Dad just came to check on me, and he brought the book *Through the Looking-Glass* with him. He found it downstairs in the library. It was the only

English book he saw on the shelf, and he was all excited about it, so I didn't tell him that I've already read it.

Actually, my Bubbi (my grandma, Mom's mom) read it to me when I was really little. And the only thing I remember about the book is that it's the sequel to *Alice's Adventures in Wonderland* and that Alice falls through a mirror into a strange world.

It wasn't my favorite book, but it's probably the perfect book for this trip, because being here is a lot like being in another world. I feel like I've landed in a wacky version of my real life.

My eyes feel dry. The light from this lamp is headache-bright. I better turn it off and get some sleep. Good night.

NOPE! It's too dark.

I tried reading some of *Through the Looking-Glass,* but now it feels a little nightmarish, with Alice and the Red Queen running as fast as they can and getting nowhere.

I'll write some more instead . . . but about what? I need a cheerful topic, the stuff that happy dreams are made of.

Actually, I kind of have to pee, but I'm sure not going to walk down that dark, creaky hallway to the bathroom *now!*

I wonder if Aunt Beth ever used her diary this way—as a shield against the dark—when she was far away from home.

Mom once told me she was jealous of her sister's diary when they were kids, because Aunt B would shoo her away and say, "Not now, I'm writing."

One time Mom heard me tell Joey to get lost when I was writing in my diary. She said it gave her chills to see history repeating itself like that. "Oh my! I've given birth to my own sister!" she joked.

Mom says she tried keeping a journal a few times, but she didn't get anything out of it. Isn't it strange that two sisters could be so different? Joey and I are light years apart, of course, but that's because he's a boy. I figure it would be different with a sister. I've always wanted one.

On the other hand, look at my mother. *That's* what having a sister can do to you if she dies! No thanks.

I wish I could totally forget Mom when I think about Aunt Beth, so I could have a private hunk of sadness all my own. But it's like Mom is hoarding all the pain, like she's grabbing all the sorrow for herself, and the only thing left for me to do is to pity her.

Does that make any sense?

date: July 15
when: 11:00 in the morning
where: Up in my tip-top room

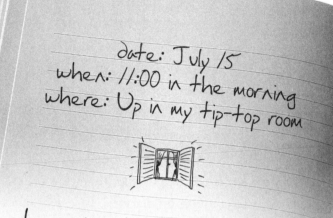

Last night Dad told me that the shutters on my window were to keep out the winter and that I didn't need to close them in July, but I'm glad I did. It was great to be able to open them this morning as if the day were a book!

Today's title page showed a moody-looking mist that reached all the way to a twinkleless lake.

I went downstairs to the first floor, following the sound of dishes being rattled. When I walked into the kitchen, expecting to find Mom or Dad, I discovered the caretaker there instead.

We both kind of jumped and squeaked at the sight of each other. Then we said good morning, each in our own language. She was putting away our dinner dishes. No one had told me she was going to be here this morning, and I wondered whether my parents knew.

She had already set the table for breakfast, using five million green and white dishes, juice in a pitcher instead of a carton, a sugar bowl, a jelly bowl, and a creamer. She even put the bread in a basket and the butter on a butter tray with a lid.

The only time we get that fancy at home is for a holiday dinner. I hoped I wouldn't have to help wash all those dishes.

I told her my name was Robyn, and she pointed to herself and said, "Katharina." Once we'd had that caveman chat, I was stumped for more conversation, so we just smiled and nodded at each other like those toy dogs with the bobbing heads you see in old ladies' cars. When the nodding got ridiculous, I left in search of my family.

I found Joey on the foot of my parents' bed, pretending to be asleep.

True, I was a little nervous last night, too, but you didn't see *me* running downstairs and jumping on anyone's bed. Joey is getting younger and younger right before my eyes. Soon he's going to become a fetus and blink right back out of existence!

He made me go with him to the bathroom and wait outside the door because he was scared to go alone. I was afraid to go last night, of course, only because it was dark and I didn't want to trip and make a huge noise and wake the whole house. Joey, on the other hand, has been sticking to everyone like gum, because of ghosts.

Please.

As soon as my parents were awake, I warned them that Katharina was in the kitchen. Then we all trooped downstairs and ate together. Not like home, where we each grab our own breakfast.

I'd never noticed how tiny my family was until I saw the four of us practically lost at that massive country table, surrounded by a sea of dishes.

Katharina had disappeared, but she rematerialized when we were clearing the table. She tried to take a pile of plates out of my mom's hands. Mom got so uncomfortable, I guess about being waited on, that she fought Katharina for them.

Once Katharina had succeeded in wrestling the dirty dishes away from my mom, she looked totally confused. I could tell Katharina didn't know what she'd done wrong. Someone had to explain to her that Mom was a little off her rocker. I hoped that someone would be Dad.

But it wasn't.

He did try to make a joke about our traditional American dish-fighting customs, but of course Katharina couldn't understand, so it didn't help.

Mom slinked away, with Joey close behind her, and Katharina ducked into the kitchen. Dad stood in the doorway and tried to use his bits of German on her to find out what the house rules are, as far as meals and things are concerned.

But I wonder what he *actually* said, because she looked even more puzzled by his German than she had been by Mom's angry dish dance.

Katharina said something back to Dad, and he thought she might have been saying that she only served breakfast and we were on our own for the other meals.

But maybe not. He said it was also entirely possible that she'd announced that the Austrian Prime Minister was expected for tea at noon. Or that if we wanted our laundry done, we had to dance on the hairy roof. Dad shrugged and gave up, then scurried off after Mom and Joey.

I rolled my eyes, took a deep breath, and tried my best to explain to Katharina about my mom. I made a sad face and mimed tears running down my cheeks. Then I said, "Her sister died."

Whether or not she understood exactly what I was saying, I could tell Katharina knew something sad was going on. She nodded sympathetically.

I nodded back. We did our nod thing for a while longer, and then I left.

I found Mom in a room with low tables and big lamps. She was curled up like a cat in a large, over-stuffed chair. I looked inside the drawer of one of the tables and discovered an old chess set inside.

The pieces were made of stone, not plastic. That reminded me of the part in *Through the Looking-Glass* where Alice is a pawn in a huge, human-size chess game.

I don't know why I asked Mom if she'd like to play. I already knew what the answer would be.

Joey piped up that he'd play me, but I hate having to constantly re-explain to him how each piece moves. Plus, whenever I win, Joey calls me a cheater and flies into a snit.

Dad came to my rescue. He made us all go out for a walk.

And WHAT A WALK!

We crossed the meadow to a little dirt path that went up and up. I could hear running water next to us, but the creek was so overgrown that it was practically invisible. It occurred to me that if I had been running through the meadow singing, "The hills are alive with the sound of music," I wouldn't have heard the gurgly splash of the water till I'd fallen in!

Nature does come up with some sneaky tricks. Hidden streams. Black ice. Things that look harmless but aren't.

Maybe that's why Mom got freaked out when we found some big, juicy blackberries growing among the wildflowers and Dad, Joey, and I wanted to taste them. Mom was sure they were deadly poison. She begged us not to eat them, but we ignored her and picked handful after handful, gobbling them down until we were purple from nose to chin. Deeeelish!

And no one got sick.

A little further up the path, we saw a chicken cross in front of us. So of course Dad and Joey and I had to tell all of the "chicken crossing the road" jokes we could think of. Even Mom couldn't help tossing one in.

The chicken clucked as if it was annoyed and shot suspicious looks at us over its shoulder. But eventually it led us to our closest neighbor—a huge farmhouse with swarms of red geraniums in flower boxes under every window. The farmer was wearing green coveralls and pushing a huge plastic barrel with milk sloshing around in it. He didn't seem to mind our looking at his chickens and geese.

We waved and smiled.

He waved and smiled.

We nodded.

He nodded. Then he invited us to see his dairy cows. He had a whole bunch, including two gangly, newborn-looking calves and one middle-aged one (or teenage—however that works in cow years). It was so sweet faced, with its silky hide and big brown eyes, that even Joey, who hates everything here, liked it. And when the cow tried to lick him with its long tongue, Joey cracked up all over the place.

Then we saw the farmer's wife. And yes, she *did* have a white cloth on her head, exactly like in the paintings! I thought, "Wait till I tell Aunt Beth!" but then I shook that thought right out of my head and hoped it didn't pop into Mom's.

There was a farmer boy, too, but he just hid behind things and peeked at us. I guess shy is shy in any language.

We learned that the cows and people actually live under the same roof here, believe it or not. Our neighbors live in the front of the house, with the pretty flower boxes, and the cows live in the back, with the hay.

Dad thinks it's brilliant. He says it snows like mad here and it would be insane to have to tromp through blizzards to feed and milk your cows—much easier to just cut through the back of the house. He wondered why American farmers didn't do it this way, why they build their barns and stables way the heck across the field instead.

I figure it has something to do with flies. There were a lot. And it didn't smell too great, either.

On the way back to our place, we saw two gigantic brown slugs with light brown spots. I thought they were interesting, but Joey was totally grossed out and terrified. He asked Dad for an "uppy"!

I told you he was growing backward. Imagine a seven-and-a-half-year-old asking to be picked up and carried. And even sicker, my dad actually did it! He lugged my stupid brother all the way back here in his arms.

when: 3:30ish
where: The room with the
overstuffed chairs

I'm exhausted! What a day.

It started out OK, with that great walk we took. But then we went for a ride. I forgot to bring you along, so I had nothing to do while we were driving. Don't get me wrong—it's not that I care that much about you, it's just that you would have helped me kill some car time.

Anyway, while we were driving, my mother told me that we were getting near where Bubbi's parents came from.

I never knew Bubbi's parents (my great-grandparents). My mom barely even knew them. The only story I remember hearing about them is that when

Bubbi gave my aunt the name "Beth," my great-grandmother, who had a heavy German accent, said, "BETH? As in BETH-TUB? What kind of a name is THAT?"

I was glad my great-grandparents left this country and immigrated to America so Bubbi could meet Zeyde (my grandfather) and have my mom, so Mom could have ME!

But when I told my parents that I thought history was great, meaning it made ME possible, Dad said, "History was far from great around here."

I asked what he meant, and he said, "In Hitler's time, the Jews in Austria had it really, really bad."

Then Mom said, "Not a single one of Bubbi's relatives survived the Holocaust."

Wow. The Holocaust, when Hitler and his Nazis killed millions of people in death camps. We've studied it a lot in Sunday school, but hearing about it on Sunday mornings in Baltimore is entirely different from being right where it actually happened. Major, major willies!

If Bubbi's parents hadn't left Austria when they did, they would probably have been killed in World War II. And without them, the rest of us—me, Bubbi, Mom, Joey, and Aunt Beth—would never have existed!

Not that it did Aunt Beth any good.

Well, that's not true. I'm sure that Aunt B would rather have had a short life (thirty-eight years) than no life at all. Right?

But why are we visiting a place *on purpose* that Bubbi's parents had to escape from? Just because Dad's airfare was paid for by his work? Wouldn't my ancestors, the ones who did and the ones who *didn't* get out in time, think that was a pretty lame reason?

On the other hand, maybe they'd be glad we came here. Maybe it would make them feel better to know that we *could*—that their homeland is a perfectly nice place to visit.

Joey started feeling carsick, so Dad pulled off the road into another scrubbed-clean, postcard-perfect town. Ho-hum. Everything is so beautiful around here that it practically makes me miss litter and pollution. (Just kidding. Well, half-kidding.)

Joey said he felt better, but we got out of the car anyway to stretch our legs. Then we wandered around, following the crumbling stone wall of an ancient castle. They sure did like to pile up rocks in the days before video.

The place was entirely silent and we didn't see a soul, except for one twitchy-tailed cat who wouldn't look at us.

After a while we found ourselves in an old church cemetery. The headstones were fancy, with intricate black iron crosses and tiny paintings on them. Aunt Beth's cemetery has all flat grave markers so the lawn mower can just zoom right across the place.

The little crumbly cemetery we saw today was *much* prettier. Plus, I bet carrying flowers to an actual headstone and telling it your problems feels a lot better than talking to a flat slab, no matter who's under it. It's just not as poetic. That's my opinion.

So whoever is reading this, if I'm dead, please give me a real headstone. That's my note to the future. (No wonder Emily says I'm morbid.)

EMILY! Hey—that's so weird!! I think this is the first time I've thought about her this whole trip. Emily's my best friend in the world. (Of course, if you were my real diary, you'd already know that.) I was sure I'd miss her to death, and now that I'm thinking about her—I do!

I can imagine what she would say about the thief who took our luggage. Emily always has wonderful curses. I think I'll write to her right now.

I can't write to Emily because my address book was in my SUITCASE!!!

I can't stand this.

Add to the stolen-items list:

1) My address book

2) My box of stationery

3) My pens (two blue, one red)

4) My markers

5) The novel *Sadako and the Thousand Paper Cranes*, which Emily gave me as a going-away gift. She said she'd loved it and cried so hard when she read it that she could hardly breathe. I was a little afraid to cry like that so I only read a few pages on the plane.

This is *not* helping. I know my aunt would say that our thief was probably really poor and had starving or sick or dying children who needed our stuff way more than we do. But that doesn't help either. His kids don't need my ADDRESS BOOK!

Grrrrrrrrr.

Back to today: Just beyond the cemetery, we came to a vineyard. And it turned out that *this* was where all the people of the town were. There was a cafeteria there, and one whiff of food made us realize instantly that we were ravenous.

All we had to do was point to what we wanted in the glass case, and while the ladies behind the counter dished out our lunch, they chattered away as friendly as can be. We didn't understand anything except their smiles, but it was easy to like them. Plus, the food looked and smelled terrific.

We carried our trays outside to a long wooden picnic table, where we had to sit with strangers. It felt a little weird, but it was OK. My parents got into a conversation with an older couple from Finland who spoke English.

Meanwhile, Joey was looking across the rows and rows of grapevines, toward a castle on the distant ridge. He shouted, "Hey! That's like Snow White's castle!" And that was the first time I got it that *this* is what Disneyland is trying to imitate.

The lady from Finland kept touching my hair. She said she always wanted to have hair that color, which is black. Anyway, now I know why you're not supposed to pet a dog while it's eating. It's incredibly annoying! If I wasn't such a good puppy, I would have bitten her Finnish fingers off.

I know she didn't mean any harm, though, and after we finished eating she suggested that Joey and I go to the play yard. When she saw that we had no clue what she was talking about, she walked us around the building to a field of pretty weeds. There were a bunch of kids playing on a tottery teeter-totter and a rusty swing set.

Joey's not a bit shy, so within seconds he and some boys were shooting each other with sticks. I wasn't sure what to do until a girl with long brown hair and a cute face said, "Hello," to me in English. "You are American, no?"

I said, "How could you tell?"

And she laughed as if I had to be kidding. But her laugh wasn't mean. She told me she was from Italy and asked if she could practice her English on me.

I said, "Sure!" and nodded, in case she didn't know what "sure" meant.

She told me that her name was Anna, or Hannah, or maybe Anya? It was hard to tell because of her accent. But whatever her name was, I liked listening to her talk. She seemed nice and she knew a lot of English, which she said she'd learned in school. Imagine!

Then she asked me if I was learning languages besides English in school, and I said, "Yeah, right," meaning "no," which confused her. So I explained that English is such a tricky language that we study it pretty much full time in Baltimore.

She'd never heard of Baltimore, or Maryland. I could tell she was a little bummed that I wasn't from New York City or Hollywood. She asked if Baltimore was near Chicago. She'd been to a wedding there when she was six.

She told me she'd arrived in Chicago on October thirty-first. When she got to her cousins' house, they were all wearing vampire and princess costumes. They gave her a big paper bag and took her trick-or-treating. As she went door to door, collecting candy from smiling strangers, she'd thought America was a wonderful country! The next night she was all ready to go out trick-or-treating again, until her cousins gave her the bad news about Halloween only happening once a year.

Her story cracked me up.

Then she asked me what my first impression of Europe was.

Even though Austria wasn't her country, I didn't want to tell her that the thing that made the biggest impression on me was getting my luggage stolen, so instead I told her about the fluffy white bathrobes and slippers at our first hotel room.

Then I was afraid that it made me sound like a typical shallow, rich American, so I added, "And I love what you've done with your dead people!" Meaning the pretty grave markers and the wacky catacombs and all that. But she just looked at me a little funny and changed the subject. She asked if I'd ever been to Italy.

I told her I loved pizza and lasagna but I'd never, until now, even been out of my own country. She was shocked until I reminded her that America is really big.

"Italy is small," she laughed. "But it is neighbors of Austria. Your family could visit!"

"It's that close?" I asked.

She gave me a look that said, "Surely you knew

that Italy was next to Austria!" How embarrassing. But what a strange idea—to just hop over to another country.

Anna (Hannah? Anya?) was really interesting to talk to, but she did make me feel kind of stupid. Especially when another kid asked her something in German and she immediately rattled off an answer, also in German. I didn't ask her how many other languages she spoke.

But it was great having someone to talk to other than Dad, Mom, or Joey.

And it sure beat writing in you, which I've been doing way too much of lately.

While Anna/Hannah/Anya and I talked, and Joey and his new friends shot at each other, and my parents drank wine with the Finnish people, the sky got darker. Huge, black clouds bubbled up behind the castle in the distance, making it look less Snow Whitish and more Addams Familyish. Cloud shadows swept across the valley of grapevines, right toward us. I'd never seen a storm approach like that before. It was amazing.

Anna/Hannah/Anya's parents called to her, and she didn't roll her eyes or ignore them or yell, "In a minute." She just jumped up and left, shouting, "Ciao, Robyn!" over her shoulder. Then she was gone. Poof!

It's weird, knowing I'll probably never see her again. I meet girls all the time back home, like in swim classes or at the ice rink, that I might not see again. But this girl doesn't just go to a different school—she lives on a whole different continent! Why does that give me shivers?

Anyway, we started back here to the farmhouse in such a hard rain that the windshield wipers, even on super-fast speed, barely parted the sea. Our puny blue rental car felt like it was surfing. Plus, the roads are just gravel and mud, and very twisty, with no streetlights.

It was scary. At least *I* was scared.

I couldn't help wondering who the Austrian doctors would call if we had a really nasty accident. I hoped they wouldn't call my Bubbi because that would be the end of her—not that there's all that much left of her since she lost my aunt Beth.

People kept telling me after the funeral that it's the most painful thing in the whole world to outlive your child and that I shouldn't expect Bubbi to ever get over it. But Mom isn't doing that much better than Bubbi, and Aunt Beth was only her sister, not her daughter.

Anyway, I decided that if we were killed on the road, it would be best if the Austrian authorities just went ahead and buried us. At least then Bubbi would be spared having to go to another funeral.

But then how would Emily ever know what happened to me? And what would they write on our graves? "HERE LIE FOUR TOURISTS"?

While I was caught up in those cheery thoughts, the rest of my family had decided we should stop somewhere to wait out the storm. So when Dad saw a sign for a bistro, he pulled over.

We counted to three. Then we threw open the car doors, jumped calf-deep into a river of swirling mud, got instantly drenched, and ran for the bistro.

But it was locked. We knocked and yelled, but no one answered.

After banging and hollering some more, plus adding a few kicks, we finally gave up.

Dad looked like a drowned rat, standing there with his sopping hair, fogged-up glasses, limp mustache, and a very strange expression on his face. When I turned away from the door to see what he was looking at, I saw nothing but rain, mud, road, and more rain.

It took a second to realize what I *didn't* see.

Then we were all screaming and splashing and slipping back to where the car was supposed to be. Peering off the road, we spotted it way down the side of the hill, tipped weirdly into the mud. And looking (at least to me) smug.

We sloshed back to the bistro and tried hammering and hollering on the door again. Nothing. So we went to the next door and yanked on the bell cord. Finally a man appeared. He was obviously deeply suspicious of wet people. And he spent what seemed to be a very long time deciding whether or not to let us in to drip on his foyer floor.

He acted like he'd never heard, much less spoken, English before and was *not* interested in starting now. Then my dad gave him a soggy five dollar bill, which the man studied closely. Finally he agreed to let us use the phone.

Unfortunately we had no one to call. I was about to suggest calling Katharina, but then I remembered that I'd never seen her with a car.

Dad decided to call a taxicab from *Zell am See*. He said he remembered seeing a couple cabs puttering around the square there the other day.

Our "host" acted like it was pure agony for him to give the cab company directions to where we were. But he did, finally, for another wet five. Then, while we waited for the cab, he stood there glaring at us to make sure we didn't step a micro-inch further into his hallway.

When the cab finally pulled up, we cheered as if we'd won the lottery and burst out of the house. The taxi driver clucked sympathetically as we climbed, shivering, into the cab and bunched up together in the backseat. He told us we were only seven kilometers from home, which Dad translated into about four miles.

The drive back to the farmhouse was uneventful, and as soon as we got back, Katharina made us tea (*tee*). She's been speaking more and more English as she gets to know us. Between that, hand gestures, and making faces, we can all communicate pretty well.

Mom took her *tee* to her room, and Joey went with her.

Dad is on the telephone, of course, with no more smiles—fake or otherwise.

And now that I'm home and dry I say: Good riddance to that dumb blue infection of a car. I never trusted it in the first place.

I'm only surprised that it didn't commit its crime when we were still in it.

time: 5:45 p.m.
place: Library window seat

The rain is dramatic and moody and broody-looking and all that, but a girl can only stare out the window for so long without going mad from boredom. Luckily, about an hour ago, Katharina rescued me from the brink of insanity.

She pulled me into the kitchen and handed me a worn-thin towel.

I'm not usually a big fan of cooking, but this was so cool that I want to write down what we did before I forget.

It started with Katharina washing a bunch of apricots. Then she showed me how to pat them gently dry, as if they were delicate baby chicks. After that, we carefully cut each apricot halfway open, lifted out the pit, and slipped an almond in its place. I loved that. It was like hiding a treasure.

Next, Katharina put a ton of butter and some white crumbly cheese (which wasn't exactly cottage cheese, but close) into a bowl.

Then she asked me how long my mother had been so brokenhearted.

"Since February," I said, holding up my hand. "Five months."

Katharina seemed to understand. She shook her head sadly. "Your heart also, yes?" she asked.

Tears instantly came to my eyes. I nodded.

Katharina handed me the bowl and spoon as if she thought it would make me feel better to smush the cheese and butter to smithereens. I think there were eggs and sugar and flour in there, too, and I don't know what else. Salt maybe.

I stirred and mashed while she watched. And by

the time it had turned to dough, I did feel better.

The next thing we did was wrap the dough like a blanket around each apricot until there was no fruit showing.

Then, PLUNK! Katharina dropped them into a pot of boiling water.

They immediately sunk.

But after a while, they bobbed to the top, just like Bubbi's matzo balls in chicken soup.

Next, we gently rolled the blobs in butter and sugar and cinnamon. Katharina let me taste one. It was unbelievably yummy. She called these something that sounded like "ka-nudel" and said they were dumplings. But these weren't anything like the dumplings I've had before, which were made of potato and tasted blah.

We lined the rest of the dumplings up in a pan, and then we put them in the oven to keep warm until dinner. I can smell them all the way here, in the library. Mmmmm!

I wonder if my great-grandmother knew how to make apricot ka-nudel. I wonder if she ever made them for my Bubbi. I know Bubbi never made them for me.

But come to think of it, Bubbi does make a *kugel* with noodles and apricots and cottage cheese. I bet it's related!

Right now the sky is as dark as midnight, even though it's only six o'clock, and the wind and rain are rattling the windows.

Maybe it's time to close the shutters.

My dad's been on the phone all this time, and I didn't notice until now that his voice is as dry as burnt toast.

when: After dinner
where: Up in my room

The ka-nudels were a big hit!

But they weren't the only treat. Right before dinner, at about six thirty, Katharina came charging into the library and told me to follow her, quick.

At first I thought that something bad had happened, like the ka-nudels had burned. But Katharina was smiling. It turned out that the rain had stopped and she wanted me and the rest of my family to see the rainbow.

It was enormous, from horizon to horizon, with each color as perfectly distinct as a rainbow bulletin-board decoration in a preschool!

I took a bunch of pictures of it. I hope they come out. Emily would die! She *loves* rainbows. And that's the kind of natural wonder I can handle—unlike, say, a GLACIER.

Which, now that we are autoless, Dad has finally stopped threatening to take us to.

Good. I hope he forgets entirely.

Dad did tell us at dinner, though, that he's going into town tomorrow to rent another car and to make arrangements for having the old one towed out of the mud. Personally, I think we should just leave it there to rot.

Perhaps my timing wasn't great, but I reminded Dad to check with the police while he was there to see if there's any news on our stuff.

He looked at me like I was as dumb as dirt and snapped, "*Forget* our stuff, Robyn. It's gone."

I knew that. But it was still like having cold water thrown in my face. And I consider myself an expert on cold water after today's soak in the rain.

But do you know what the feeling reminded me of? It reminded me of when I had to undo all the lies that adults kept telling Joey when we were "sitting shivah" the week after Aunt Beth died.

(Isn't "sitting shivah" a strange thing to call sitting around and mourning? It's a Jewish custom, and I think it has something to do with sitting on hard chairs—as if you need a reminder that being sad is uncomfortable. But our family doesn't follow Jewish law that strictly, so we made do with our sectional sofa.)

Anyway, first I'd heard my cousin Barbara, who's three years older than me and should have known better, tell Joey that Aunt Beth went on a long trip. Someone else told him that Aunt Beth was asleep. Then Bubbi's old friend, Pearl, from the bridge club told Joey that God wanted Aunt Beth with Him because she was special.

Those were just the things I heard people say. Who knows how many bizarre things they told him that I didn't overhear?

I pulled Joey into the bathroom and said, "Listen, Aunt Beth isn't on a trip and she's not asleep. She is DEAD. She's not coming back and she's not waking up. Got it?"

Joey scowled at me. "Leave me alone," he said.

But I made my brother look at me. "God did *not* take Aunt B because she was special. Special people *and* totally worthless people die every day. Pearl was lying."

"You're mean!" Joey said and stomped out of the bathroom.

I sat on the toilet lid and asked myself if my brother was right. But I decided, no, I was being kind and big-sisterly.

Because what if Joey actually believed that Aunt Beth was just sleeping? Wouldn't he worry that she'd wake up and find herself underground, alone in a coffin? Plus, if we buried Aunt Beth while *she* was asleep, Joey might wonder what would stop us from burying him while *he* was sleeping! He'd be so scared that we'd never be able to make him go to bed.

And if Joey thought Aunt Beth was on a trip, wouldn't he wonder why everyone was crying? Or at least ask when she was coming back, and why she didn't say good-bye or send us one of her usual funny postcards?

Then I was mad at my parents for not talking to my brother about all this. And for telling him instead that he was a big, brave boy for not crying. I was mad at them for not bringing him to the funeral so he could see for himself.

But I was especially mad at my parents for leaving the dirty work to me. I think that's when I realized that everything had changed for me, somehow. Not only was my auntie gone, but a part of me was gone, too. I wasn't totally a kid anymore.

It's not very classy that I had my realization while sitting on a toilet seat, but oh well.

And now, five months later and halfway around the world, I know how Joey must have felt when I told him that Aunt Beth wasn't coming back.

Anyway, we ate the apricot dumplings at dinner, and everyone loved them. Dad patted his belly and said, "Butter, sugar, dough—what's not to love?"

The dumplings were so melt-on-your-tongue delicious that they even seemed to warm Mom up a bit. She let Katharina help in the kitchen tonight. No wrestling match over dirty plates!

Magic ka-nudels???

date: July 16
time: 9:45 in the morning
place: Zell am See, at a cafe
table on the square, under a
yellow-and-white-striped
umbrella. Alone.

Dad is in the building across the street, talking to the car rental people. It was nice of him to invite me along with him this morning, and it's kind of exciting being here by myself like this, but he's been gone for an awfully long time.

I already ate my rolls and drank my hot cocoa. Now I'm sipping my water with gas (that's what they call sparkling water) as slowly as possible to make it last until Dad gets back, so the waitress won't tell me to leave.

I wish Dad would hurry.

Still, as long as the car rental people give him a much bigger and better car so that I won't have to sit so close to Joey anymore, it'll be worth the wait. And you never know, but maybe the delay is because they found our stuff!

I know I'm not supposed to hope that anymore, but hey, I'm only human. Right?

Ugh! It's starting to drizzle again. My shoes are still squishy with *yesterday's* rain and mud.

Wow! The clock tower over there is dated MDXXI. I didn't notice that when we were here the other day. Ms. Lipson would be horrified to know how long it just took me to figure out that the Roman numerals say 1521. I can't imagine anything being that old!

It means there's nowhere on this entire square, I bet, that a girl could walk (or sit drinking fizzy water) that many, many girls haven't walked or sat before. And some of those girls probably wore corsets and long dresses and had crushes on boys who wore capes and carried swords!

Dad was in a rotten mood during the taxi ride into town. I think the car slipping away may have pushed him over the edge, too. (Ha! A pun!)

I shouldn't have complained about Dad being so cheerful before. It sure beat the way he is now—grouchy.

And I wish he hadn't left me just sitting here like this. I don't even know the phone number at the farmhouse, or where it is, exactly.

And now it's raining again and the town square isn't nearly as cute without the flapping laundry. Plus, I don't speak the language and what if I need a bathroom?

What's taking my dad so long? I've had it. I feel stupid sitting here. I just want to go home. Not to the farmhouse, but *home*.

And if I really had my way, I'd not only go back to our apartment but *all* the way back to the time before the accident, when everyone was still themselves. When the only dead person I knew was my downstairs neighbor Steven and my biggest problems were math problems.

I've been trying to make the most of this trip, but it's hard. If I were home, Emily and I would just be hanging out. We'd go swimming with our friends Allison and Sabrina. We'd sleep over at each other's houses. I wouldn't be with my family every second of every day like this. It's unnatural.

And I want to see normal stuff, like malls, signs in English, and not so many white people. Back home, everyone is everything. In my class we've got Korean, Armenian, African American, Japanese, and Latino kids. Joey's class has Chinese and Filipino kids. But here everyone looks related to one another.

Why didn't we go somewhere regular for vacation? Someplace easy and fun, like Florida, instead of a place with endless rain and piled-up bones, where the water has gas and the meatballs are made of liver.

Who needs a place that's haunted with memories of the Holocaust, where everything is so old and dreary, and where luggage gets stolen? Well, scratch that last part. Luggage gets stolen back home, too. But why couldn't we have gone to a normal, English-speaking vacation spot in our own country, like Emily's family does?

Actually, Emily is going to the Grand Canyon this summer, and I wouldn't want to go there. (Heights and edges are not for me, as you know.) So forget that, but I'm sure there are a lot of other places to go right near home.

If we'd done that instead, I wouldn't be huddling under this umbrella, abandoned in a foreign country, in the rain.

I know, I know, I *know* that it's pointless to think about what would have happened if what did happen *didn't*. But if I'd stayed in the United States, you'd still be in the stationery shop in Vienna.

Or maybe you would have been sold to somebody else by now. Maybe an Austrian auntie would have bought you for her niece! And that niece would love writing all of her own secrets and confessions on these pages.

Plus, my old diary would be safe in my hands—not in the garbage somewhere covered with moldy banana peels and greasy fish bones.

That diary had my Aunt Beth in it.

No other diary ever will again. Not ever.

I'll never forget when I first got it. Aunt Beth *made* me pay attention.

There were a lot of other Hanukkah presents to open, and Joey and I were tearing through them. But when I got to the one wrapped in brown paper (Aunt B's trademark), she made me slow down.

After I'd opened it, we looked at it together. And we talked about it.

Who would have believed that just two months after she gave it to me, I'd be using that diary to write about her death? And that just five months after *that*, I'd be using *another* diary to write about losing the first one!

You know how just a few days ago I thought that maybe if someone nice found my diary and read it and cared about me, then it wouldn't be that bad? Well, forget it. That's a total crock.

Where the heck is my dad?

I hope that before we go back to the farmhouse he'll take me shopping here in town. I need to buy Emily something. I don't know what, but something Austrian and pretty. She's the best friend I've ever had, and I owe her something wonderful, whether she knows it or not.

Here's why: A couple of years ago, when Emily's grandmother (she called her Nana) died, I just didn't get it. Nana was old, and she'd been sick for years, so I didn't see what the big surprise was when she died. I thought Emily was just acting sad to be dramatic and get attention. It annoyed me.

I was scared of Emily's church and the funeral home and death and sad people and all that, so I skipped the whole thing. My mom said she'd take me, but I just couldn't make myself go.

Emily never said anything about what a lousy friend I was, so I thought maybe it didn't matter.

Then Aunt Beth died and Emily showed up at the chapel, even though a Jewish funeral was probably as scary and strange to her as I thought a Christian one would be.

I don't remember seeing Emily at the memorial service. There was a big crowd, and I didn't notice much of anything, in fact—other than the casket.

It was as smooth and shiny as Bubbi's dining room table. I wondered if it was as nice on the inside. In the movies they always show half-open coffins so people can say good-bye, but Aunt Beth's was closed up and had a candelabra with burning candles on top of it.

For one giddy moment I wondered if this was all a big hoax and maybe Aunt B really ran off to Tahiti. How could I possibly be expected to believe she was in that box?

But everybody around me certainly seemed to believe she was. They filed past us to give their condolences, looking like one long, swollen, red-eyed snake of sorrow.

I didn't think about Emily on the drive to the cemetery, either. I had always wanted to ride in a limousine—of course, not like that. Not with my Bubbi moaning beside me, and my mother pale and trembling next to Dad.

And not following a hearse with my Aunt Beth dead inside it.

Although the crowd had been huge at the chapel, not that many cars lined up for the procession to the cemetery. But among the group that braved the weather to huddle around my aunt's graveside was Emily. There she stood, shivering in the freezing wind with her dad.

The rabbi hurried through the Hebrew blessings, because of the cold. And then he started to lower my aunt's coffin.

Bubbi had been moaning all along, but then her moans grew to a wail that mixed with the whistling wind. That was all I could hear until my cousin

Sandy led Bubbi back to the mourner's limo.

With Bubbi gone, I could suddenly hear the squeak of the ropes and pulleys lowering my aunt's casket into the grave. And I could hear Mom, next to me, making deep animal noises, something like growls.

It scared me.

Until the accident, it had never occurred to me to worry about my parents dying. But now I knew that if my cute, fun, totally *alive* auntie could die, then anyone could.

I was afraid for my mom, and I was afraid for myself, too, wondering if the pain in my chest was a junior heart attack.

The rabbi threw a shovelful of dirt into the grave. It hit Aunt Beth's coffin with a thud.

Then my mom shoveled some in. Thud.

Then Dad. Thud.

Then me.

Other people, Aunt Beth's friends, barely recognizable through scarves and hats, lined up. One after another they shoveled dirt into my aunt's grave, then hurried off to their cars.

Soon almost everyone was gone. But not Emily and her dad.

The weather got even worse. The wind ripped at our coats and stung our faces. But the coffin still showed, light pine through the dark dirt.

My family believes in the Jewish custom that you shouldn't leave the graveside until you've laid your loved one to rest—meaning that the coffin has been completely covered up.

So we kept shoveling.

Mom threw one shovelful and another and another. Then she got frantic and started shoveling faster and wilder until she stumbled.

We all gasped, imagining what would happen if she tumbled in. Thank God my father caught her. He took the shovel out of Mom's hands and gave it to me.

I dug a scoop of dirt and hurled it into the grave. Dig, throw, thud.

Again. Again. Dig, throw, thud. Then Emily reached for the shovel. Her father took a turn next. And then me again.

The only sounds besides Mom's gulping sobs against Dad's chest were our raspy breaths, panting white clouds in the cold air, and the grim thud of the dirt. My tears were freezing and re-freezing, but I'd actually started to sweat from shoveling.

I'm sure Emily and her dad were sweaty, too, but they didn't leave until we were done.

It took a long time.

A really long time.

You need an enormous amount of dirt to cover a casket. I can still see that dirt. And I will always hear that sound.

Here comes Dad. FINALLY.

when: 10:20 a.m.
where: On a bus that runs
between towns

(Fact: There isn't one bit of litter or a single doodle of graffiti anywhere on or in this bus.)

Dad did *not* get another rental car. He has to go all the way back to Vienna to get one! *And* he has to pay the towing charges for the old car, because it was totally his fault that the car rolled away. Turns out he'd forgotten to put the parking brake on. (OOPS!)

So we're taking the bus home from *Zell am See*. We think it has a stop somewhere near the farmhouse. (We hope.)

People keep getting off in the middle of nowhere. How can they tell which stop is theirs in this endless sea of soggy farmland?

Dad was snarly with me. He wouldn't take me to a single store to shop for Emily. And when I asked if he'd happened to hear anything about our luggage, he practically bit my head off! Excuse me, but was I the one who forgot to put the parking brake on?

Oh, great. It's starting to rain even harder, and I swear I can feel the bus swishing from side to side.

I wonder how close we'll get to the farmhouse.

time: 11:15 a.m.

Answer to the above question: not very close. There was much uphill trudging through mud with a grumpy dad and sopping shoes that weighed at least fifty pounds each.

Now, however, I am above it all—in my room at the top of the house. Under the blankets.

Sick of:

#1. My entire family.

#2. Wearing the same two outfits (one Austrian and one Baltimorian) over and over. I wish I'd worn one of my new outfits to the Emperor's Palace the day everything was stolen. Then again, if I had, it too would be all muddy and stretched out or shrunk and unraveling by now.

#3. Rain. It is no longer a thrilling, crashing, oh-wow storm. Just a ho-hum, boring gray drizzle.

I bet that over the last three hundred years, a lot of people have been bored to death listening to the rain in this exact same room. I wonder if any of them ever actually died up here.

Died to death.

OK, now I've given myself the willies. I wish I was home in my own room, in my ghost-free, modern American, history-less apartment!

Oh. That was a chill going up my neck. My apartment building isn't so history-less. Aunt Beth was there just moments before she died.

She had come to pick up my mother for the dance concert. They invited me to go along, and I definitely would have, but I was in a panic studying for a huge history test that I was afraid I was going to flunk.

Bubbi was staying with me for the evening. My father was at the gym. I don't remember where Joey was—probably at a friend's.

I wish I'd paid more attention so I could remember that last visit with Aunt B better.

Actually, what I really wish is that I had put down my books and talked to her—about *anything*. If only I'd kept her and Mom out of Miss Sweetness Brown for just a little while longer. Five minutes? Ten? It might have made a difference.

But all I remember is that I was sitting at my desk when Aunt Beth came in and flicked my ponytail hello. I hope I said hello back. I hope I smiled, at least. But I'm afraid that what I really did was wave her out of the room, saying something like, "Can't talk. Gotta cram for a big history test tomorrow."

Of course, I didn't end up taking that test the next day anyway because, well, you know why.

Update: I went looking for my family and found them all standing around the front door with Katharina and a tall man who looked familiar. For one glorious second I thought he was the Viennese policeman, here to deliver our lost luggage.

When Dad saw me, he said, "*Here's* Robyn!" as if he'd been searching high and low for me. "Rob, you remember Mr. Lieben from next door?"

And then, of course, I realized that the man was the farmer with the cows and chickens. He just wasn't wearing his farmer get-up this time, and he hadn't had a name before.

Dad explained to me that Katharina had kindly arranged for our neighbor to drive Dad to the train station, because there were no buses that would get my father there in time, and cab fare was starting to add up.

All this made perfect sense, but Dad looked like he'd rather be eaten by alligators than accept the ride.

I peeked out the door at the farmer's truck. It looked fun to me. Riding in that great big thing would have been heaven compared to our puny rental car!

Go figure.

Dad told us that the train would get him into Vienna this evening. He said he'd spend the night there and be back sometime tomorrow afternoon or evening—with a new car.

I said, "Get a red one."

"No, get yellow!" Joey said. "A convertible!"

Dad shrugged, peeled Joey off his leg, and kissed each of us. Then he headed out the door with Mr. Lieben. His last comment to me was, "Take care of your mother."

Take care of my mother? Excuse me, but aren't mothers supposed to be the ones taking care of the children?

We watched my dad and Mr. Lieben slosh through the puddles to the truck. Then Dad splashed back to promise us that as soon as he returned, we'd go to the GLACIER.

Oh goody.

My dad got in the truck and waved good-bye while Mr. Lieben tried to start the engine. It took two or three times to turn over, but finally the truck gave a hop and took off. Mr. Lieben honked the bullhorn as they turned and rattled down the hill and out of sight.

I looked at Joey, who was near tears, and Mom, who just stood there expressionless. Her blankness is really getting on my nerves. I'm nobody's mother, but even I know that when a kid is sad that his dad has left, you're supposed to pat his head, at least. But Mom no longer pats heads.

I came back up here instead of yelling at her.

Eewww, Dad going back to Vienna, land of luggage thieves. *Double eewww* for us, stranded in this great big house in the endless rain.

This is hard. There have been cool parts of this trip (although I can't think of any right this second), but mostly I feel sort of clenched and ready to duck all the time. Like I'm out here with no protection, no one looking out for me, and anything could happen.

Oh yeah, "anything" already happened.

Dad said the thief only took our *things,* and he claims it's good for us to see how little we really need to get by. ("A change of socks, a sweater if it gets cold," he says.) But Dad's wrong. The thief stole way more than just our things. He took every drop of hope out of this vacation.

time: 4:30 p.m.
feeling: Groggy

I guess I fell asleep and dreamed (or half-dreamed, half-remembered) the drive to the hospital the day Aunt Beth . . . I hate all the ways of saying it.

"Passed away" sounds so vague and drifty, and my

aunt wasn't the drifty type. "Left us" sounds like she had a choice. "Lost" as in, "that's the day we lost Aunt Beth," sounds dumb, as if we left her on the bus. And "was killed" is way too violent. I guess that leaves plain old "died."

The day Aunt Beth died.

I didn't hear Bubbi get the call from the hospital. Suddenly she just started yelling to me to get in the car. I was studying, so I yelled back "Not now" or "In a minute" or something.

The next thing I knew, Bubbi was dragging me out of my chair as if I were a bag of laundry. Then she shoved my coat at me and pushed me out of the apartment without my scarf or boots.

Thinking about it now, I'm surprised she didn't just jump in the car and take off without me.

At first I was more confused than frightened. But then I saw how bug-eyed Bubbi looked, straining to see out the unscraped windshield through patches of caked snow and ice. She was driving like a lunatic, skidding all over the road and muttering.

That's when I got scared. I kept asking what was wrong and where we were going, until finally she said, "My babies. Oh, God, please—not my girls!"

That sunk in. She meant MOM. Something was wrong with my mother! I wasn't even thinking of Aunt Beth at that point.

We turned in at the hospital. Bubbi lurched to a stop where a sign said "Ambulances Only." She bolted out of the car, and I had to scramble to keep up with her, slipping on the ice. I chased her through the automatic doors to the emergency room and saw her grab the sleeve of someone in a white lab coat.

Just as I caught up to her, another white lab coat came out and asked Bubbi if she was related to Debra Gittleman or Beth Levine. Then he said Debra was doing fine but there was nothing they could do for Beth. Collision. Ice. No airbag. Wreck. He was sorry.

Then I watched the doctor very s-l-o-w-l-y catch Bubbi, who was sort of melting. Then he s-l-o-w-l-y turned and called to a nurse to bring a wheelchair.

My entire world went into slow motion. I don't know how else to describe it. The doctor even blinked slowly. And it took hours for me to move my eyes from the doctor to Bubbi in his arms. I wondered why Bubbi's face wore such a strange, twisted expression.

It took an eternity for me to understand that Bubbi had collapsed. That my mother was alive. And that this man was saying that my aunt Beth— was *not*.

I went searching for my voice, which seemed to be lost or hiding somewhere inside me. I had to explain to this doctor that he was terribly, terribly wrong about my aunt. It was almost funny how completely wrong he was. But I couldn't remember how to get sound to come out of me.

Eventually I managed to say that I'd just seen my mom and my aunt and that they were both fine— going to a dance concert in Miss Sweetness Brown. And Miss Sweetness would never let anything bad happen to them.

Then I was sitting on a hard green plastic chair, and someone was telling me they were sorry. I didn't understand what they were apologizing for.

Next, Mom was there, all bandaged up and holding Bubbi. Or Bubbi was holding her, or both.

The rest is dim. I don't remember how we got home from the hospital. Did Dad come? But then there would be two cars there. And when did Joey show up? Or did he? It doesn't matter. None of it matters, really.

I hate how my brain just springs these memories on me anytime it wants. Like falling on the ice. I'm walking along, minding my own business, and suddenly my feet zip out from under me, schoolbooks fly, arms fling around trying to grab the air, and— BAM! I'm on my butt.

I wish Emily were here. First of all, she'd love Austria. She'd be thrilled by this house and the furniture, the meadows and cows, and even, probably, the rain. She'd be wild about the indoor swing. She'd love the old-fashioned bathtub.

And secondly, she'd be *here* if she was here. (Duh.) And I'd catch her happiness as sure as catching a cold. And we'd have fun, and I wouldn't be so screamingly lonely!

What's wrong with me? Why aren't I as happy here as I know Emily would be? Am I just an old grump or what?

when: After dinner

At around five o'clock I went downstairs and found Katharina building a fire in one of the fireplaces, which was the perfect thing for a drippy gray day like today.

I curled up in the window seat with *Through the Looking-Glass* and read the part where a gnat asks Alice what kind of insects they "rejoice in" where she comes from. I thought about the huge brown slugs we saw yesterday, although I'm not entirely sure if slugs are insects.

Then (in the book) the gnat sighs and sighs himself away, until he actually disappears!

Right on cue, I heard Mom sigh in the hallway. She came into the room, took one look at Katharina, and in a really cold voice, said, "Please stop that!"

Katharina froze, fireplace poker in mid-poke, and looked at Mom.

Mom said, "We cannot afford servants. I don't know who you think we are, and I don't know what the Müllers told you about us, but we can't possibly afford to pay for all your attention."

Katharina put down the poker and wiped her hands on her apron. "No pay," she said, shaking her head. "I do because I want. Yah?"

Mom got flustered. She looked at me, I guess for help, but what did she think I could do? "That's very kind," she tried again. "But it is not necessary. We will manage on our own."

Katharina put her arms out as if she was going to hug my mother.

Mom looked startled and stood stiffer and stiffer as Katharina moved closer to her.

I interrupted. "Katharina? We aren't used to help. I think it makes my mother uncomfortable."

"I try to make more comfort! I try to ease pain."

"Pain?" Mom asked.

"About your baby. Such terrible sorrow." Katharina held her arms as if she were cradling an infant and moved further toward Mom.

"What baby?" Mom's voice was getting higher. "What are you talking about?" She looked at me, wild-eyed. "Where's Joey?"

Joey popped his head out from behind a chair.

Then Katharina looked confused, too. She turned to me and said, "Your sister?" And I finally got it.

"Oh!" I said, giggling. "She means Aunt Beth!" I pointed to my mom. "*Her* sister, not *my* sister. I never had a sister. I meant my aunt! My mom's sister!"

Katharina still looked confused, but I could see her translating my words in her head until she finally smiled a little. "Ahhh . . ." she said. "Still very sad, a sister." Then she added tentatively, "But not terrible like baby. Yah?"

I wouldn't have thought Mom could get any stiffer, but she did. "My sister and I were very close," she hissed.

"Of course, terrible sorrow. I have sister, also," Katharina said, nodding. "And I love. But beautiful daughter, to lose this would be biggest sorrow, no?"

Mom blinked at Katharina. Then she looked at me, as if she'd forgotten I was there. I thought I saw a light flicker in her eyes, sort of like a computer screen when you first turn it on.

Mom reached over and pushed my hair off my forehead. It had been so long since she'd done that, it made my forehead tingle. Then she touched my cheek and I could barely breathe. I told myself *not* to get my hopes up, but too late—they were UP! My mother was back!

Out of the tiniest corner of my eye, I saw Katharina nod again. Then she said, "I make tea," and left the room.

Mom put her hands on my shoulders. "You do know how much I love you, don't you, Rob?" she said. My hopes climbed even higher—right up my throat, almost choking me, almost hurting. But I stood still and bit my lip to keep from saying anything that would scare her away.

Then, imitating Katharina, Mom said, "Sister nothing like baby." And from the way she looked into my eyes, I knew she meant it. I was afraid to move, not wanting to wreck the moment.

But the moment self-destructed anyway.

Mom's eyes filled with tears. She took her hands off my shoulders and, in her nobody's-home voice, said, "Beth would have gotten a kick out of Katharina, don't you think?"

Mom was gone. I mean she was *there*, right in front of me, but the light had gone out again. The screen was blank. I was disappointed down to my toenails. Disappointed, discouraged, deflated, and all those other hopelessly empty-feeling *D* words.

The rain continued to piddle down the window like tears.

Just as I was about to sigh, I remembered the gnat sighing itself totally away. I didn't want to be a gnat.

Plus, I realized that my disappointment was my own stupid, pathetic, unrealistic fault. I'd practically asked for it!

Of course Mom wasn't just going to snap back to her old self, like a cartoon character after being flattened by a steamroller. Real life isn't like that.

I'm not going to get my mother back in one whopping, magic-moment BANG!

I suppose it's possible, though, that I might get her back in a lot of little BINGS, added together. Maybe this was one of those bings. I guess I can handle that—as long as the bings keep coming.

For the rest of the evening I pretended that I was Emily, because pretending to be interested in things, like she is, made *me* sort of interested. For instance, I noticed that Katharina's roaring fire made the room feel like the center of the universe.

I played a million rounds of tic-tac-toe with Joey, and I even let him ask me his annoying knock-knock jokes for the tenth time. He makes up his own, such as:

Knock Knock.

Who's there?

Maca.

Maca who?

Macaroni! (That's when I'm supposed to keel over laughing.)

And guess what! When Katharina brought us tea and crackers, Mom asked her to sit down and join us. (Bing?)

After dinner (leftovers in front of the fire, including a couple of reheated kanudels), Joey fell asleep on the floor. I helped Mom carry him to her room. She said that as long as Dad was gone for the night, she'd let Joey sleep with her. She told me he'd been having nightmares and ending up in their bed every night anyway.

I said good night and came up here to crawl under the covers and write in you.

Wow! Listen to that thunder. And the lightning is wild. I don't think there was any lightning before, was there?

This old house must have stood through a lot of grizzly weather in its life, so I'm sure it'll be fine.

But what would we do if it was hit by lightning?

If we were in flames, would the farmers up the road notice? We can't see the Liebens' house from here, so they can't see us. And they wouldn't hear a thing over this wind. But maybe their shy farm-boy son would look out of his window and see smoke curling up.

Would it be too late to save us?

I don't want to die so far from home.

That sounds dumb. I mean, I don't want to die at

home, either. But I wouldn't even want to go to the hospital with a splinter here.

It's weird not having Dad in the house.

When: Later
Where: In bed, getting freaked out

Well, *that* didn't work. I tried to fool myself into going to sleep by pretending I was Emily, but I guess that trick doesn't work for everything.

Plus, who knows how brave Emily would be up here alone in the dark, in a three-hundred-year-old farmhouse in the middle of nowhere, across the world from home, during an electrical storm, with her dad gone and her mom down two flights of stairs and sort of useless anyway?

I know I could pick a different bedroom tomorrow night, one closer to everyone. And I'm pretty sure no one would laugh at me for doing that.

But I'm not going to. That would be weak. That would be quitting. That would be, I don't know what that would be, but I'm not going to be whatever it is.

The problem is that with the light off, this room is so dark that it's impossible not to wonder if it's any darker in a coffin underground. And then I feel guilty for being spooked by dead people when my own Auntie B is one of them.

I think I'll read *Through the Looking-Glass* for a while. It's a weird book, and it keeps going back and forth between fun-crazy and just plain crazy-crazy. But it's all I've got.

date: JULY 17th
time: ???

I guess I must have fallen asleep with the light on last night.

When I woke up this morning, I opened the shutters just a sliver and peeked out at another gray rainy sky. So I went back to bed.

I can't tell if I slept a few more minutes or all day. No one has come up to find me, so it must not be very late. I left my watch down in the bathroom last night, and there's no clock in this room, which feels strange.

I've never woken up in a room without a clock, because Aunt Beth is—was—in the clock business. She designed and sold clocks.

Now that I think of it, most of her clocks were very *Through the Looking-Glass*ish, meaning wacky.

Every room in our house has at least one weird clock, and they are constantly switched for newer, weirder ones. The one in my bedroom at the moment has tiny cranks that raise and lower numbers to tell the time. (Hard to describe.) The one in Joey's room has all the numbers backward and in the wrong places. Aunt Beth thought that was a hoot. She said, "Good luck learning to tell time, Uncle Joe!"

Last January Aunt Beth took me to a gift show in Dallas. That's where she sold her clocks to store owners who came from all over the globe. The whole gigantic place was packed with vendors selling one cool, oddball thing after another. From floaty pens to furry purses to glass chairs. I bought earrings for Emily there. They lit up and laughed like lunatics.

Aunt's Beth's booth was always crowded. People stopped by to chat and be introduced to me. Men flirted with my aunt, and everybody wanted to see what new clocks she'd come up with.

Before that trip, I'd never been to Texas, so Aunt B insisted we wear cowboy hats the whole time and call each other "Pardner." I'd spent the night at her apartment a million times, but we'd never gone on a trip, just the two of us, before. So you can imagine how fun it was. No, I guess you can't.

Well, we had a blast, calling room service, eating cheesecake and onion rings on the big hotel bed, and making fun of the stars on late-night TV talk shows. That seems like fifty years ago.

HEY!!! I don't know what took me so long to remember that I WROTE MY ADDRESS ON THE INSIDE COVER OF MY DIARY!

Maybe, just possibly, do you think some kind soul might take pity on me and mail it back? Would anyone do that?

That would be amazing, to come home from the airport and . . . TA-DAH!

Richard is taking in our mail while we're here. He'll ask us about our trip, and while Mom and Dad are talking to him, I'll hunt through the stacks of envelopes and magazines until I find the package. I'll rip it open, and there will be my diary, safe and sound. I can practically feel the cover in my hand right now.

Maybe the person who returned it will have enclosed a note so I can write back and say thank you, thank you, THANK YOU!

And I won't go back and use the rest of the pages. I'll leave them blank as a sort of memorial to the time that was lost. The diary will stay exactly as it is, and I'll keep going in you.

I think I'll go downstairs and see who's awake. And get my watch. I feel naked without it!

time: 9:48 a.m.

I found my mother at the kitchen table doing absolutely nothing. I made all kinds of noise, clomping down the wooden stairs, but Mom still jumped when I came in the room. Why does she *do* that? It's so annoying.

I guess I was secretly hoping that last night's flash of sanity was going to return today. But no such luck.

I don't know, maybe I'm just mean. Maybe I'm a bad daughter, like I was a lousy friend to Emily when her Nana died. Maybe I'm a rotten niece. I know it's only been five months, but I feel like shouting, "C'mon, Mom, get over it already!"

Anyway, Joey was in the window seat with his new action figures, making shooting and grunting sound effects. I got a bowl of granola and sat down across from Mom. The spoon was halfway to my mouth when my memory hit another icy patch, and OUCH! I was flat on my back.

This one was about that awful week when we were sitting shivah.

I know one thing. I couldn't have gotten through sitting anywhere on anything if I hadn't had my diary. I wrote constantly, as people—mobs and crowds and throngs of people—came and went from our apartment. They'd just appear, looking sad, and they'd say sorry, sorry, sorry, as if they'd killed Aunt Beth themselves.

Eventually, though, they'd be laughing and joking like it was a party. I know they didn't mean to seem unsympathetic, but then they'd see their friends and start chatting or whatever, and that was that.

I couldn't help hating those people for having fun, for being alive, and for not being my aunt.

Then I heard one guy say, "If you want a big funeral, you've got to die young. Otherwise, your friends beat you to it."

Whoever he was talking to answered, "Yep. The more funerals you go to, the less people there are to go to yours."

And although they weren't talking to me and probably didn't even know I was listening, I cracked up. *Way* up—with hysterical, uncontrollable, snot-dripping, snorting, rib-aching, cheek-cramping, not-breathing laughter. I had to duck into the laundry room to get a grip on myself.

It was true. Aunt Beth's funeral, in spite of the ice storm, had been so big they'd had to use speakers to broadcast the eulogy out into the crowded hall.

Here's what else I remember about sitting shivah. Besides telling jokes and lies, people also brought heaping trays of food, including cakes and nuts and candy. Joey, of course, was thrilled about that.

Dad was trying to keep our lives normalish, but he really had no idea how, because Mom had always been the one to manage the day-to-day stuff. Now, though, she sat slumped and dazed, and she forgot completely about being our mother.

That meant there was no one to tell Joey to quit stuffing his face or to go brush his teeth or take a bath or go to bed or change his underwear.

I tried, but it wasn't my job, and Joey never listens to me anyway.

He ate himself sick.

Actually, Joey wasn't the only one. Someone had brought dried figs, strung like beads on a rope, and I wasn't even aware I was eating them until I'd finished every single one. My jaw ached from chewing, and I got an awful, cramping stomachache that lasted the whole night.

But by far the worst thing about the week of shivah was Bubbi.

Luckily someone was feeding her pills, so she was mostly doped up and hidden away in my parents' room. But every few hours the medication would wear off, and I'd hear her moaning.

Then Bubbi would get louder and start pleading with God, begging in a bone-chilling chant, "Take me instead! Please, God, bring back my baby and take me!"

It gave me the shivers. Aunt Beth was already buried, for heaven's sake! Did Bubbi really think God would switch them?

I had to put a pillow over my head until someone would rush in and drug her again.

My cousin Sandy, who had come in from Minneapolis for the funeral, caught me once with my fingers in my ears. She smiled a sad shivah smile at me and said, "Bit much, listening to your grandmother, huh? But who can blame her for trying to bargain with God again?"

I didn't know what she meant by "again."

Sandy explained that way back when my great-grandmother (Bubbi's mom) was dying, my mom came down with rheumatic fever. Sandy said it was a total nightmare for Bubbi, having both her mother and her daughter so desperately ill at the same time. Bubbi was torn between wanting to go to the hospital to be with her mother and wanting to stay at my mom's bedside.

"Actually, she wasn't that torn," Sandy said, "because when your baby is sick, there's nowhere else you want to be than by your child's side, and there's nothing else that matters."

So that's when Bubbi prayed to God asking that if He *had* to take one of them, to please take her mother and spare her child.

And He did.

When I asked Sandy if she thought Bubbi ever felt guilty about that, she looked surprised by my question. "Of course not," Sandy said. "Your Bubbi knew that her mother would have made the same choice. It's the natural order of things."

Bubbi no longer begs to die, at least around me. But she isn't exactly living anymore, either. Other than going to temple every day to say prayers for Aunt Beth, she doesn't do much else. No more book club. No more volunteer work. No bridge. No nothing. And she's skinnier every time I see her, so she's obviously not spending her time eating.

One of the reasons I'd been looking forward to this trip so much was to get away from Bubbi and her constant pain. I know that sounds really mean, but it's true.

When I was done having my shivah flashback, I was surprised to see that my bowl of granola was empty. I didn't remember eating it. Joey's action figures were still shooting each other, but they'd moved from the window seat to the floor. Mom was staring out the window.

I followed her gaze to see what she was looking at. Nothing. A nice view of the orchard, but there was nothing happening in it. Nothing stirring but the trees.

I said, "Mom?" and she jumped, as usual. Then she looked up at me with that puzzled expression of hers. "Mom," I repeated, "where are Aunt Beth's diaries?"

My mother's eyes wandered back out the window. "In the steamer trunk in the basement."

Oh. I'd figured that trunk was full of clocks and dishes—the stuff we'd sorted through when we emptied out Aunt Beth's apartment.

That was another totally awful time. I'd hated going through my aunt's things, sorting for charity, picturing her clothes on strange bodies and her sheets on strange beds. Eeew.

Anyway, then I asked Mom if she was ever going to read the diaries, and she looked at me like I was nuts. So I guess not.

"Can I read them when we get back?" I asked.

Mom said, "No." Then she changed it to, "Maybe when you're twenty-one." And then she added, "It could be a real can of worms, you know."

I didn't know.

"Well, Beth may have written things that would upset you or confuse you, and she won't be there to explain."

I got the funny feeling that there was something Mom wasn't telling me. Like maybe she'd once sneaked a peek into Aunt Beth's diary and not liked what she saw. Serves her right, I thought. But I didn't mention my hunch. Instead I said, "Please can I read them when we get home?"

Mom shuddered and said, "Honestly, Robyn, I can't imagine why you'd want to. People can write anything in a journal. Hurtful things that may not even be true. Or they might write when they're mad at someone and say mean things in anger. And then maybe they don't remember to erase them or cross them out later."

Now I knew Mom was hiding something. I didn't push it, though. "You don't erase or cross out," I explained. "Aunt Beth herself told me *never* to go back and edit."

"See?" Mom said, nodding at me as if I'd made her point. Then she said, "Beth had no warning that her time was up. Maybe if she'd known, she would have destroyed her diaries so no one could read them." Then Mom turned away to stare out the window again.

I'm sure she was wrong. Aunt Beth had been keeping diaries since she was my age, and she'd saved them *all*. No one accidentally moves dozens of diaries from apartment to apartment and saves them for all those years just to destroy them.

I guess that's the difference between a diary keeper and a non-diary keeper. I'm sure I'd *want* my diaries read after my death. It would be almost like living a little longer.

Joey has just come up here to bug me. He's trying to get my attention, trying to read this over my shoulder. What a gnat. I know he misses Dad and just wants someone to play with, but that's not my job, is it?

when: Exactly noon, but you can't tell by looking out the windows, because it's a wall of gray. You can't even see the lake or the mountains.
where: Back upstairs, supposedly getting dressed.

I was an angel and played on the swing with Joey until Dad finally dragged in, looking all used up. He tried to greet us like his old cheerleader self, but no one bought it.

Still, the whole house let out a sigh of relief at the sight of him.

I told Dad we'd been going bonkers being cooped up inside, and I pleaded with him to take us some-where. But he said he was beat and he just wanted to sit perfectly still.

I showed no mercy.

Joey begged, too, until Dad finally said, "OK, OK. Let me just wash up and we'll go take a look at that glacier."

WHAT?! That was *not* the field trip I had in mind. So I said, "No, not *today!* This isn't a glacier kind of day."

"Well, we're running out of time," Dad said. "We only have two more days left here, and we don't want to miss our chance. How often do we get to see glaciers in Baltimore?"

Well, #1) We see glaciers in Baltimore exactly as often as I'd like to, which is never.

And #2) I don't want to be a wimp, but even the word GLACIER sounds big and old and cold. More like a giant sleeping grizzly bear than something you go driving up to for a family picnic. You don't make loud noises or poke it with a stick. You don't sneak up on it for a peek. You just tiptoe quickly away. Yah?

I finally convinced Dad that it would be way better to see the glacier on a sunny day, or at least on a day when we could get an earlier start.

"OK," he said. "But tomorrow is glacier day, rain or shine!"

Oy.

So today we're going to a town that Katharina says is beautiful. It's called *Mondsee*. She drew us a pretty little map of how to get there. She even sketched in landmarks and sights along the way and included a picture of a parking brake as a reminder. (Hee-hee.)

I better get dressed.

time: 7:34 p.m.
place: Library

Now, that was what I would call a nice (but wet) Austrian day.

Here's how you say "Austria" in Austrian: "Osterreich." Joey thinks that means the national animal is the ostrich, which is kind of funny, but don't tell him I said so.

Anyway, back when we were leaving the house, Katharina gave us each a huge black umbrella that looked like something out of an old movie. Then we walked around to the side of the house, and, ACK! There was the horrible blue rental car. Risen from the dead!

Or from the mud, at least.

Dad laughed when he saw the look on my face. He claims that it's a totally different car. He says it's just the same kind and color because that's all they have at the rental place.

But if you ask me, that is *worse* than having Stupid Car Number One back again. This one is its evil twin come for revenge!

I changed my mind about wanting to go anywhere. But Dad made me. When I got in, I swear I heard the car snicker.

I kept my eye on the road and my hand on the door, ready to jump out if the car started doing anything suspicious. Luckily, Mondsee wasn't very far away.

When we got there, I forgot all about Stupid Cars Number One and Two, because Mondsee was so cute it made my eyes water.

The little downtown was a walking street. (No cars allowed. Ha!) And each pretty storefront was a different color, like a box of assorted mints. At the end of the street was a tall yellow church with two skinny spires.

When we went inside, we saw shiny black altars trimmed in tons of gold. There were brochures in English and a lot of other languages explaining the history of the church. I took an English one to read and a couple of Russian and Chinese ones just for souvenirs.

The pamphlet said that the church used to be a monastery. It was founded (I'm copying this) by the Duke of Bavaria in the year (here's the cool part) 748. That's all. Just three numbers. Not seven*teen*-forty-eight, which would have been plenty old, but seven-*hundred* forty-eight!

Joey wouldn't go inside. He says he's seen enough churches and they freak him out because they're too dark. But I think it's really the sad, looming paintings and statues that spook him, and I can't say I blame him.

So Dad stayed outside with Joey. Dad, by the way, seems pretty much back to his old chipper ways now that he's got another stupid blue rental car.

After the yellow church, we went looking for our usual schnitzel lunch, but restaurants only serve meals at certain times here. This wasn't the first time we discovered that everything was closed between when they thought we should eat lunch and when they thought we should eat dinner.

Bakeries, luckily, are more open-minded, and we found one that looked like it had been there since the beginning of civilization. It had dark wood walls, a sculpted ceiling, a glittery chandelier, and, most importantly, brass and glass pastry cases stocked with more yummy treats than I'd ever seen in my whole life—including the dessert table at my cousin Matthew's Bar Mitzvah.

At the sight of the eclairs, though, I braced myself. I was sure that as soon as Mom spotted them, she'd say something about how much Aunt Beth loved eclairs, and then she'd slide away from us into her funk. But she didn't. (BING?)

So we sat in the bakery and watched the rain and gorged on sweets. Mr. Health Club (Dad) said it was the best lunch of his life. He had whipped cream in his mustache.

When we were as stuffed as four couches, we opened our big black umbrellas and wandered—make that waddled—through town to the lake. This was a different lake than the one we can see from our farmhouse.

In spite of the fog and rain, people on the other side of the lake were shooting a cannon into the water. BOOM! We don't know what they were celebrating, but the sound was loud and low and I heard it more with my big, full belly than with my ears.

The sound bounced through the mist and sent a bunch of geese swimming over to our side. Dad bought a roll and split it in half for Joey and me to feed them. Joey, of course, went into a snit claiming that Dad gave me the bigger half, which was total baloney.

The rain got harder, pocking up the surface of the water, but the geese didn't care. They were too busy fighting over every crumb of our roll. Dad said that's how you can tell they're siblings.

I don't know if I rolled my eyes for real or just in my head, but I thought, good going, Dad. Mom is finally acting halfway normal and you go and mention *siblings*. Now she's going to get all limp and weepy.

And right on cue, my mother turned her back on us and wandered away.

But a few minutes later, while I was concentrating on throwing bread crumbs past the greedy, loud-mouthed goose in the front to the loser in back, my mom returned—with four fresh rolls, one for each of us. The geese and I couldn't believe our luck.

By the time we walked back up to the car, it almost felt like we were a normal family on vacation.

We came home and took turns taking baths. Dad built a fire and we sat around it, bundled in blankets with towels on our heads. Joey fell asleep immediately. Dad and I played Twenty Questions, and Mom even piped in with a question now and then (bing!). I know it won't last. I'm not getting my hopes up just to have them stomped on again. But it was still nice.

And the rain stopped just in time for a spectacular silver and orange sunset, with bright, fast-moving clouds over the far hills. The library windows are the perfect sunset-watching spot.

time: 11:08 p.m.

I should have slept in a different bedroom every night. I don't know why I was being so stubborn and

115

let all these other rooms go to waste!

Right now I'm trying out a room on the third floor that has two beds. The nightstand between them is an old milking stool. I told Joey that if he got scared tonight, he could come into my room instead of waking Dad and Mom.

Tomorrow is our last day here before we go back to Vienna. My chest tightens up just thinking about being there. We'll spend one night in the city and then leave for home the next morning.

It's hard to believe this trip is almost over, after all those weeks thinking about it and planning it. But it also feels like I've been here a long time—like most of my life.

Tomorrow I *must* take pictures of everything!

But tomorrow is also Glacier Day.

When I said I thought we'd already gotten close enough, seeing the glacier from the road, Joey called me a scaredy-cat. He says I'm afraid of more things than he is. I was about to smack him when I suddenly wondered if that might be true.

If I list everything I'm afraid of about the next few days, it goes like this:

1) The glacier
2) Driving to and from the glacier (in the rain with Dad at the wheel)
3) Vienna, return of the luggage thief? (even if

there's hardly anything left to steal)

4) The airplane ride home (crashing)

5) Getting home and not finding my old diary in
the mail

really late (or early): 4:51 a.m.

I'm wrapped in my blanket, sitting in the window seat, trying to be super quiet because Joey's asleep in the other bed.

Who knows what he'll remember about this trip. He doesn't seem to notice much besides his new action figures—which aren't even Austrian. They're the same plastic, pinheaded muscle men you can get at the mall back home.

What do I remember from when I was seven? That was five years ago.

Well, that's when I met Emily. And I think that's when I started taking piano. No, maybe I was eight.

I know that for my eighth birthday, Aunt B took me to high tea at a fancy tea house. They served us tiny sandwiches and scones, and there were purple flowers on the table. I remember that my teacup had a little brass strainer of its own to catch the tea leaves. Even the napkins were lacy and girlie. My aunt and I were all dressed up, and we acted like elegant English ladies, holding our pinkies in the air.

Afterward, parked in Miss Sweetness Brown, we made all the grossest puking, belching, farting noises and said the rudest and most obnoxious things we could think of—to balance out our proper ladylikeness in the tea house.

Funny how memories like that can make me want to laugh and cry at the exact same time.

Aunt Beth won't be there for my next birthday. She's never missed one before. Even when she was traveling, she always made it back in time for my birthday. Joey's, too. Will he remember that? Will he remember being Uncle Joe?

There will also be the first Halloween without Aunt Beth doing my makeup and stealing my Kit-Kat bars. It'll be depressing to have all my Kit-Kat bars to myself.

Maybe I'm too old for trick-or-treating anyway.

I think I better go back to bed and start this day over later.

date: July 18
time: 6:22 a.m. (too early)
place: In the car, on the way
to you-know-where

The best thing about all that grayness and rain we had is that it makes a clear sunrise like this one seem extra wonderful. You can tell that the sky just woke up and hasn't pulled all its blue together yet, and the clouds are the palest pink. It's exactly as if the world is still groggy—awake but still dreaming.

Joey is half asleep, too. His head keeps bobbing over to my side, but I'm not shoving him away. Isn't that kind and mature of me?

The white dots in the fields (sheep) have long shadows. We're passing sleepy little villages nestled in quilts of farmland. But looming over each one, like the shadow of Dracula, is a massive, dark cliff. Don't the villagers hate having all that cold rock breathing down their necks? If I had a mountain towering over

119

me all the time, it would give me the permanent willies for sure.

Why does the entire world think the Austrian Alps are so beautiful? I mean they're impressive and hard to ignore, but that's not the same as beautiful, is it? Since Joey, the scaredy-cat of scaredy-cats, called *me* a scaredy-cat, I don't want to say the mountains here look scary—but they do.

We're going to pull over at the next place we see for breakfast. Let me gaze into my crystal ball and predict what they'll have on the menu. It's coming to me now: I see schnitzel, sausage, dumplings, and omelettes.

when: After breakfast
where: In the car (again)

My psychic abilities are amazing! Except I forgot to mention sauerkraut.

I also didn't predict that the restaurant would have a gigantic thing for kids to climb on that was shaped like a ship, with masts and decks and even rigging and portholes. It was swarming with little kids. Joey was halfway up to the crow's nest in a heartbeat.

He was having such a blast that I almost very nearly came close to joining him. I told myself that even if I looked like a total baby playing on it, I'd never ever see any of these people ever again, so who cared what they thought?

Well, I guess I care.

I couldn't do it. My feet wouldn't take me over there. I just sat like an old lady with my parents while they drank coffee and waited for our food to arrive. But it wasn't a total waste of time, because I learned this: Aunt Beth liked GLACIERS.

Mom was trying to make conversation (bing!), and she asked Dad and me if we remembered when Aunt B went on an Alaskan cruise.

I didn't. It must have been a long time ago.

"Beth loved it," Mom said. "She kept telling us we should go sometime, remember?"

Dad nodded.

"And remember how she wanted to paint her living room to look like the towering walls of ice she'd seen?"

I was so dumbfounded by Mom's chattiness that I just shook my head. Although, come to think of it, I do remember a blue wall in one of the apartments she lived in when I was little.

"But Beth just couldn't get satisfied with the color," Mom went on. "She thought that maybe if she cranked up the air conditioning past freezing, the effect would be more realistic." Then Mom *laughed.* (Double bing!)

121

It wasn't her industrial-strength, tropical-bird laugh or anything, but it was better than crying or just freezing up.

I was sure Mom's concentration would break, ending the spell, when Joey returned from his voyage at sea and wiggled into the booth. But she kept talking! She said that Aunt B had met a crew member on her cruise who told her that glaciers were like cows. He explained that when hunks of ice break off and go crashing into the sea, it's called "calving," like birthing a calf. And the whitish water right around the glacier is called "glacial milk."

Dad and Joey and I were grinning hard at Mom, with our eyes bugging out and our heads bobbing in a "Yes? Yes? Go on!" kind of way.

Mom looked up at us. But then she dropped her eyes to her lap and said, "My sister made friends everywhere she went." She sighed like a gnat and got quiet again.

Dad tried to keep up the conversation. He said he wondered how the local cows feel about having glacier parts named after them. And Joey made up a few exceedingly lame knock-knock jokes about milk and cheese. Don't ask.

It always makes me feel bad when Mom deflates like that. But all things considered, it was a pretty good set of bings.

Right now I'm wishing we'd gone to the stupid glacier way back when we first found out about it. Then it would be over and done with by now. Plus, all this talk about glaciers has made a mountain out of a molehill. Or out of an ice cube. Or whatever.

There was an ice storm the day that we buried Aunt Beth.

I remember waking up early and hearing bells. Tiny, tinkling bells. I had no idea what it was. Some kind of sign from Aunt Beth? Like the little wind chimes she kept on her apartment balcony?

Then I looked out my window and saw the plum tree in Richard's garden bending so far over that the top branches were practically touching the ground. Every inch of the tree, from its trunk out to its tiniest twig, was completely coated in crystal-clear ice. It looked like a beautiful, enchanted princess, bowing low in a frozen fairy-tale curtsy.

The branches, clinking together in the breeze, were making the wind-chime sound.

I watched them twinkle and listened to their music until suddenly—CRACK! The tree split in half, right before my eyes.

One big part crashed down to the ground. The rest sprung up and waved wildly, shivering and shimmering and tinkling louder than ever.

When we were leaving for the funeral chapel, we

passed Richard outside. He was standing there staring at the broken tree.

"All that ice was too heavy," he muttered to us. "Poor thing just couldn't take the weight."

Later that night, when I tried to remember the funeral service, instead of seeing the rabbi beside my aunt's coffin I saw Richard beside the splintered plum tree.

And instead of the rabbi's Hebrew prayers, I heard the tinkling of icicles.

One day during shivah, when Bubbi's tranquilizers wore off and I needed to get away from her moaning, I grabbed my coat and ducked outside. I was shocked to see that although it had been only a few days since the funeral, the world looked totally different. The sun was shining. It had melted the ice completely away without leaving a trace. Not even a puddle. It didn't seem possible that we could have had such freakishly cold weather just days before.

I noticed a fresh pile of firewood stacked by the garage. I went around to the front of the building, and yes, the fallen half of the plum tree was gone.

I saw, too, that Richard had painted the gash in the trunk with some kind of tar, to help the wound heal, I guess.

Dad says we're lost and we'll have to stop in the next town to ask for directions.

Later:

The village we stopped in was called *Hallstatt,* and boy am I glad to be leaving it, although I'm sure I'll never forget it as long as I live! Not because the village is (no kidding) *four thousand* years old. And not because of how pretty it is, with its steeply sloping roofs and wooden balconies.

But because of the SKULLS.

We went into one of the church buildings to ask for directions, and somehow we ended up crowded into a hallway with a family from Ireland. They were friendly and spoke English but with such a thick and funny accent that it was almost impossible for me to understand them.

English and *not* English at the same time! I felt like Alice after she'd slipped through the mirror.

I wondered if Irish people read *Through the Looking-Glass.* Then I remembered that the book was written in England, so actually, people in Ireland probably got it way before we did. Maybe they were wondering if *we* knew about Alice, all the way across the ocean.

In any case, suddenly I was staring into the empty eye sockets of dozens of human skulls!

The skulls were decorated and pretty, painted with flowers and ivy and names and dates in fancy lettering, but still—THEY WERE SKULLS! Real skulls. The kind that used to be in real heads.

The Irish family explained it to us. They said there's no room in the town for graves because the whole town is sort of backed up on its tiptoes—with all the buildings holding onto each other for dear life—against the edge of a (brrrrr!) glacial lake.

You gotta wonder why people ever decided to dangle their town off the edge of a mountain, on such a wee strip of land. (Notice the Irish *wee*.) Why not just settle somewhere else? I mean, the view was spectacular and all, but still.

Anyway, the solution that the Hallstattians (Hallstatters? Hallstoids?) came up with was to bury the dead for a while, then dig them up, paint the people's names and dates of birth and death on their skulls, and keep them on display as a memorial!

Except they (the people who are still alive) don't save the lower jaw. So the decorated skulls sort of look like they're biting the wooden shelf that they're sitting on. And underneath the shelf, the rest of the bones are stacked tightly, as neat as firewood. Imagine!

If I hadn't seen it for myself, I would never have believed it.

I guess the Austrians just aren't as grossed out by their dead people as we are. In the United States, something like this would freak everyone totally out. My aunt's cemetery doesn't even like head*stones* showing—let alone *heads!!!*

After we'd had all the bone-gazing we could bear, we went with the Irish family to have pastries and cocoa.

I had to shove the image of those dusty, jawless skulls out of my head in order to swallow. I kept picturing the food going right through where my chin should be and falling on the ground.

Dad told the Irish people that we were heading for the glacier, and it turned out they'd already been.

The boy, who was halfway between my age and Joey's, said the glacier was boring! That was the best news I'd heard in days. And I could feel myself getting a wee crush on the lad (or is it laddie?) in spite of his wee age.

The boy said that once you got up to the glacier, it was just like being in a gigantic field of snow. (Actually, that sounded semi-cool to me, in July.) And he said the only good thing about it was the ride up there.

Gulp!

Then he said that even *that* wasn't so great because it's a mammoth gondola (which is a fancy way to say cable car) that holds around twenty people, so it's too big to swing.

SWING???

Joey looked at him with pure admiration for even *thinking* of swinging a gondola that was hanging by a thread, a zillion feet over the pointy Alps.

Then everything really turned ugly when the boy told us that what was much better than walking *on* the glacier was walking *inside* it. In the (get this) ICE CAVES!!!

Oh, please.

I don't think I ever switched from liking someone to detesting him so fast in my entire life. Our thief was Prince Charming compared to this twerp.

But Dad and Joey loved the idea of ice caves, and even Mom said it sounded interesting.

I HATE interesting! I said that, and everyone laughed as if I was joking. Which I wasn't.

So now we're on our way there. And we're close. I already saw signs for the Ice Cave Café.

I admit it. I'm afraid. I don't care if Joey calls me "scaredy-cat" twelve times a day, every day for the rest of my life.

Dad just smiled at me in the rearview mirror and said, "There's nothing to worry about, Robyn. It'll be fun!"

Yeah, right.

Oh, no! We're here!!

Help!!!

place: Farmhouse (by the fire)
time: After dinner, recovering from
our Adventure on Ice

PHEW! We're alive.

Well, I knew it would be horrible, and it was way worse than I'd feared.

But like I said, we're alive.

How should I write this? Backward? Forward?

OK, here's what happened. They gave each of us yellow coveralls that went from ankle to chin, and miner's lamps to wear on our heads. That was a big hit with Joey, and I admit I kinda liked it, too.

But then we went inside the cave and a door closed behind us.

The cave was awful. Well, at first it was *only* awful. It wasn't like a hallway or a room, exactly, because it was weirdly shaped. Not to mention gigantic and solid ice. It didn't feel as much like being in a building as it felt like being in the mouth of some huge frozen creature.

Then we started down the creature's throat, single file, on narrow, slippery, rickety wooden stairs. Some parts had a railing to hold on to, some didn't.

Most of the other people in our group were part of a huge bus tour of retired people from Japan.

They gasped and giggled as they clutched at each other and carefully made their way down the icy staircase.

I giggled, too, at first. But mine were nervous giggles, not happy ones. Dad was behind me, and he tried to hold my hand, but having my arm twisted backward felt even less safe so I let go.

There were *a lot* of stairs, and they were steep. It wasn't the least bit fun, and I just wanted to get OUT—but on we went. The air was cold and stale and creepy.

And the worst part, at least for me, was knowing that we were getting deeper and deeper under the ice, a million miles from normal life.

Then we were crowded onto little boats. (Who knew there was even water down there!) We bobbed past gigantic ice stalactites and stalagmites.

When I learned those words in science, I never suspected I'd actually use them. The formations looked like giant, pointy teeth. And they were lit purple and green, which was extra weird. We drifted between them for what felt like endless, twisty, underground miles.

Then our boat bumped to a stop, and we climbed out and started back up the stairs. I'm not sure if these were the same stairs we came down, but they were just as icy and narrow.

I wasn't hearing any tourist giggles, happy *or* nervous, anymore. And I noticed that Joey was no longer calling anything neat or cool. Only my dad was still pointing and saying, "Oh, wow! Will ya look at that!"

But I didn't look, because by then I practically had my eyes shut, willing myself out of there. I was starving for fresh air and daylight.

We were almost to the top when, somewhere on the stairs above us, there was a scream and then echoing screams. And suddenly, everyone was shoving and falling. I was knocked down.

The lights on our heads shot crazily, every which way. It was total confusion.

As I struggled to get up, I felt like I was moving in slow motion, as if the air had turned into slush. I wasn't hurt, but I was totally scared and rattled.

I looked around. I wasn't the only one having trouble. Some people were trying to get up, while others were just lying there, either yelling for help or crying.

I saw Dad's legs slip out from under him as he tried to stand. And I couldn't do anything but watch. Finally he was on his feet, and he pulled me and Joey up, too. Then he was hugging us, and Joey was crying.

I searched around for my mother.

It took my eyes an eternity to sort through the confusion and focus on Mom. And another eternity for my brain to understand that Mom was cowering on the icy steps, about halfway down, with her hands over her face.

Even over all the other cries for help, I could hear her low animal growls. And I realized that she was back in time, frozen in terror inside Miss Sweetness Brown—with my aunt dead or dying beside her.

I saw Dad turn and start to make his way down toward Mom, but there were too many people in his way. Plus he was still holding on to Joey, who was wailing his head off.

I stopped hearing everything else around me, or thinking about the ice, or the cave, or the glacier, or any of that. All I could think was that if my mother didn't spring back up, like the plum tree, she might be lost forever.

My world snapped back to normal speed.

"I'll get her," I yelled over Joey's shrieks.

Then I skidded and stumbled down the steps to where she was lying and practically fell on top of her. I grabbed her arm and yanked on it. "Come on, Mom. Get up."

But she just curled up tighter.

I bent down and yelled, "Mom, c'mon! You have to get up!"

I tried to peel her hands away from her face, but they wouldn't budge.

"Dad needs help with Joey. Please, Mom, we've gotta get out of here!"

Finally, slowly, she dropped her hands and looked around.

Dad tried again to start down the stairs toward us, but I waved to let him know we didn't need him. He nodded and turned around, carrying my totally freaked, wild-eyed brother out of there.

Mom sat up. Then she took my hand, and we helped each other stand. Carefully we began creeping back up the slippery stairs to the light.

When we got to the top, we just stood there, gulping air. Dad, with Joey in his arms, made his way over to us, and the four of us swayed for a while in a big hug. Joey's wails finally simmered to whimpers.

Dad had learned that the whole accident had been caused by one guy slipping on the stairs and bowling over everyone behind him.

Suddenly Mom broke away and turned back toward the mouth of the ice cave. We could still hear shouts coming from inside.

"Debby!" Dad said. "What are you doing?"

"They need help," Mom called back over her shoulder.

Was she *nuts?*

Then I realized she wasn't nuts at all—she was being *normal!* She was being her regular, fighting, take-charge, same old SELF!

My real mom was back.

Then I was the one who acted a little nuts (for me, anyway). The last thing I wanted to do was go back down into the cave, but somehow, being separated from Mom again seemed even worse.

So I hurried after her.

She tried to stop me, but I refused to go back to Dad and Joey. I told my mom that if she could do it, I could do it.

She looked at me with one of those what-am-I-going-to-do-with-you smiles, and shook her head. Dad shrugged helplessly, still holding my squirming brother. Then Mom took my hand.

Together we made our way carefully down the stairs. The first people we came to were an elderly couple. The woman was sprawled out on a step, and the man seemed exhausted from trying to lift her. After we helped him hoist the woman to her feet, Mom went off to help someone else.

I was left with the terrified couple clutching on to me for dear life. I was afraid we were going to fall and start the whole snowball over again. But what could I do? We didn't speak the same language, and I couldn't just pluck their hands off me. So we went slowly—very, very, slowly—up those icy steps as an awkward threesome.

When we finally reached the top, the old man bowed to me.

Dad and Joey took over from there, leading the couple to a bench.

I ducked back into the cave.

My eyes searched below me for my mom. There she was, supporting a stooped, frail-looking man as he made his way up the stairs. Her face was glowing. Her eyes actually looked bright! I almost hugged myself. But instead, I sort of hugged the little old lady who was clinging to me. She wasn't hurt, but like the others, she'd had trouble getting up and was scared.

It only took a few more trips to get everyone else out of the cave. By that time, the medics had arrived and were treating people for injuries.

Dad was assisting them, and even my brother helped by sitting and talking to people. They probably didn't understand a word Joey said to them, but they nodded at him as if they could tell that he was a nice boy. Maybe he reminded them of their grandsons back in Japan.

The man from the Ice Cave Café passed out hot cocoa to everyone. And it was kind of strange—people were still shaken and scared, but after a while the whole thing felt like a celebration.

In the car on the way home, all four of us felt pumped up and proud. We were soaked to the bone and shivering, but we were happy.

It turns out that Little Blue Rental Car Number Two has a great heater. And once we got off the mountain, we realized it was a warm day, so we rolled down the windows and finished drying in the wind. The sunny breeze and sweet green scenery, after all that ice and fear, made us giddy.

Now we're back at the farmhouse. Joey got the first bath, and he's been in there for ages, singing a song that he made up about what a hero he was today. His favorite line must be "He's the bravest boy on ice. Oh, that Joey is so nice!" because he has repeated it about forty-eight times.

Anyway, when Katharina heard our story, she offered to make us a good dinner. I expected Mom to grumble, but she just said, "Thank you. That would be wonderful." (BING!)

And it was.

I could swear I just heard Mom say, "Robyn, Joey's out of the Beth-tub. It's your turn." Was I imagining things, or did she just make a joke with the word *Beth* in it?

This is even weirder: Mom just said, "It's nice to hear you laugh, Rob."

I said, "Huh? ME?"

And she said, "Yeah. You've been so quiet and serious lately."

Now is that as backward as Alice's looking-glass world or what?

when: Bedtime, last night
in this house
where: In the bedroom with
the swing

I'm not saying that I'm even the teensiest bit glad all our stuff was stolen, because I'm not. But here's what I know. If we'd stayed in Vienna, going to palaces and museums and stuff, I'd never have sat in a three-hundred-year-old window seat or thrown open shutters.

And if my diary's not waiting in the mail for me when I get home, I'll be bummed, but it won't be the end of the world. The important thing is I had it when I really needed it.

Not that I don't need a diary anymore, just that maybe it doesn't have to be *that* diary.

Speaking of diaries, Joey tried to read you for the nineteenth time after dinner tonight, but Mom caught him. And guess what—I was right about her having her own diary-spying experience.

My mother told us that when she was younger, she wanted to be a singer. She used to stand in front of the mirror and belt out songs as loud as she could, with plenty of emotion. She thought her neighbors would enjoy it and, who knows, maybe a passerby would discover her and make her a star.

One day, even though my mother knew that it was wrong and criminal and an invasion of privacy and all that stuff, she snuck a peek into Aunt Beth's diary and read, "Debby is in the bathroom right now, caterwauling like a screech owl again. I wish somebody would tell her how absolutely dreadful she sounds!"

Mom said she was insulted and embarrassed and angry and hurt, but there wasn't a thing she could do besides stew. She couldn't confront Beth, or she'd have to admit she'd been snooping. The worst part, though, was that it took all the fun out of singing, Mom said. She didn't really sing for years after that, and then only in the shower.

Mom looked sad for a second, but then she cracked a grin and chuckled, adding, "I've been cringing over that for more than twenty years! Isn't that silly?"

I didn't say it, but I was thinking that Aunt Beth did my mother and the whole world a favor. I've heard my mom sing in the shower—not lately, of course, but I used to—and caterwauling like a screech owl sums it up nicely.

But Joey, if you're reading this, I just want you to know that Mom's singing voice is a chorus of angels compared to *yours!*

Ha!

date: July 19
time: 10:11 a.m.
place: A beautiful Austrian farmhouse surrounded by alpine meadows. (This is the last time I'll be able to write that!)

I spent the whole morning running around snapping pictures of everything—the armoires, the wildflowers, even the milking stool and the giant bowl in the dining room. I hope they come out. I can't wait to show Emily and tell her everything!

This may not sound like much to you, but Mom just came in here (the room with the swing) and actually *yelled* at me to get the sheets off the bed and into the wash! She even said, "Put down that diary right now and get moving!"

It was like hearing a ghost. It's been ages since my mom yelled at me, and believe it or not, I missed it.

I must have gaped at her with my tongue hanging out, because then she said, "What are you staring at?

We've got to get moving!" Then she walked out as if nothing shocking had just happened.

It occurs to me that my old diary had my mother in it, too, not just Aunt Beth. You will never have Aunt Beth in you, but maybe you can have some of my mom. My real mom.

She just poked her head back in here to say, "Robyn, I told you to put that diary down and strip the sheets off your bed!"

Then she didn't know why I burst out laughing.

where: New hotel room in Vienna

The farmhouse already seems an impossible number of light years away, and it has only been a fistful of hours since we left.

As we headed down the hill, I said, "Good-bye, farmhouse."

Joey said, "Good riddance." Then he stuck his tongue out at it. What a turkey! The whole experience was wasted on him.

I didn't write in you on the drive here because it was my last chance to look out the window and see all the corn and wheat and cows and sheep.

We stopped in one last village to use the bathroom, and I bought the cutest apron with a dairy cow design for Emily. I hope she likes it.

Now we're back in Vienna. This hotel has a parrot in the lobby who speaks German and laughs like my mom. And the woman behind the desk keeps giving me and Joey these incredible chocolate candies. Plus, our room has an awesome view. No lake or meadow or mountains, but miles of rooftops with weird chimneys and red church spires and a huge blue-green dome.

And it's not raining!

As soon as Dad gets off the phone, we're going to the Ferris wheel. I'm not exactly looking forward to it, but after the ice caves, I figure I can handle anything.

when: Bedtime
where: Hotel room

That Ferris wheel made all earlier Ferris wheels seem like the kiddie ride at a backyard carnival. But a girl in our gondola, who was even younger than Joey, saw me turning green and advised me not to look down.

That didn't make the ride any more *fun,* exactly, but at least it kept me from fainting or puking.

And now I can say I DID IT.

Ice cave disasters? No problem. Monster Ferris wheels as tall as skyscrapers? Handled.

Tomorrow's flight across the ocean in a piece of metal? No sweat.

Emily won't even recognize the new fearless me.

After the Ferris wheel, we took the Müllers to dinner at a Chinese restaurant to thank them for letting us stay at their farmhouse. The food didn't taste like Chinese food at home, but it wasn't terrible and it wasn't schnitzel and the Müllers liked it.

We talked about the meadow and the window seats and the green-and-white loopy dishes. And we talked about Mondsee, the town with the yellow church, and Hallstatt, the one with the painted skulls. And, of course, the ice caves.

Joey sulked the whole time, and when the Müllers asked him how he had liked the farmhouse, he shrugged one shoulder and looked away.

I wanted to clobber him for insulting the Müllers after all they'd done for us. I quickly changed the subject, hoping they wouldn't notice what an ungrateful turd my brother was.

I said, "And Katharina was very sweet. I really liked her."

"Who?" asked Mrs. Müller.

"The caretaker lady," I said.

Mrs. Müller looked at Mr. Müller.

"Ah!" Mr. Müller said, leaning forward. "I have heard of Katharina. My great-grandmom saw her, and also my grandmom. My own mother claims she has seen Katharina and even baked dumplings with her. But this mother of mine"—Mr. Müller crossed his eyes and twirled his finger to make the international sign for cuckoo—"she has many flights of fancy."

For one creepy moment, I felt a chill run down my spine. But then, without letting Joey see, Mr. Müller flashed me a wink.

"I TOLD you the place was haunted!!" Joey cheered, knocking his chair over. "Told you so! Told you so!"

Still feeling a spooky tingle, I wondered if this was the kind of joke that liverball and blood-sausage eaters think is funny.

But then I decided it *was* funny, and I smiled back at Mr. Müller. I would have winked but I don't know how.

Joey couldn't be happier. Now that he thinks the farmhouse was haunted and that he met a real ghost, he loved it there.

Anyway, tomorrow we fly back to Baltimore, which seems as unreal to me now and hard to picture, as Austria was before the trip.

I'm sure you'll like America, and you'll like my room. I'll be keeping you on a shelf next to my bed, where I used to keep my old diary. And if my old diary is waiting at home for us, don't worry. There's plenty of room for both of you.

I'll miss having a window with shutters to throw open, but at least I can see the plum tree from my room. In the spring it had blossoms on it again. And who knows? By the time we get back, maybe it'll be full of plums.

Meet the Author

Amy Goldman Koss

Then

Now

As a girl growing up in Detroit, Michigan, Amy
Goldman Koss always kept a diary. She saved those
journals, and to this day she loves to embarrass herself
by rereading the entries. Amy came up with the idea
for *Stolen Words* on a recent trip to Europe with her
family, during which all of their luggage was stolen.
They didn't let it spoil their vacation, however, and
Amy fell in love with Vienna and the Austrian countryside. Amy is also the author of several popular
children's novels, including *Smoke Screen, The Girls,*
and *The Ashwater Experiment.* She lives with her husband and two children in Glendale, California.